Treachery at Twin Forks

When Marshal Rick Farnam foiled an attempted train robbery he little suspected the crime was only part of a much larger conspiracy. The town of Twin Forks was a powder keg just waiting to explode, and in the middle of it all was Ed Jordan, a cunning rancher who, aided by a crooked sheriff, was scheming against the smaller ranch owners.

Fearing for her father's life, rancher's daughter Anne Dancroft turns to the marshal for help. Now, as Jordan makes his attack with renegade Apaches in his ranks, Farnam must face the greatest danger of his career. But would he survive to taste victory?

Treachery at Twin Forks

Edmund Cordell

ROBERT HALE · LONDON

First published in Great Britain 2005

ISBN 0 7090 7807 2

Robert Hale Limited
Clerkenwell House
Clerkenwell Green
London EC1R 0HT

Typeset by
Derek Doyle & Associates, Shaw Heath.
Printed and bound in Great Britain by
Antony Rowe Limited, Wiltshire

CHAPTER ONE

HOLDUP!

The railroad from Dawson Bend ran westward for more than 1,000 miles before it reached California. In the early afternoon sunlight, the gleaming metal rails shimmered in the oppressive heat. It was only four years since the railroad from the east had met with that stretching from the western coast. Now there was a single track spanning the entire continent.

That afternoon there were only three people waiting for the train. A stout man dressed in a long black coat and hat, was carrying a large bag which he never let out of his sight. There was a nervousness about him which was immediately obvious.

A tall, slender woman in her mid-twenties stood a little way back from the rails. She had an overnight bag with her. From her clothing it was clear that she had spent some time back East.

The third passenger was seated on the low bench against the depot wall. He had ridden into Dawson

Bend the previous day, a tall man with a hard, weather-beaten face. Now he sat with his head drooping forward on to his chest, almost asleep. From his appearance it was evident that, some time earlier, he had drunk more than was good for him.

He scarcely stirred as the whistle sounded in the distance. Not until the train pulled in did he lurch unsteadily to his feet, oblivious to the disapproving looks of the other two. Somehow, he climbed into the carriage where he slumped into the seat at the end.

Five minutes later, the train pulled out, the wood-burner throwing a large plume of black-and-white smoke into the still air.

Halfway along the carriage, Henry Jepson, a banker from New York, sat tensed in his seat, white-knuckled fingers clutching the bag on his knees. He was headed for Twin Forks to take charge of the bank there and rather than risk the two-day journey by stage, had decided to take the railroad.

The bag in front of him held more than $5,000 for the bank. Even the thought of all that money made him sweat. He took out his handkerchief, mopped his face and wiped the perspiration from his eyes. This was still lawless country and he wouldn't feel totally safe until the contents of the bag had been deposited in the bank vault.

Almost immediately behind him, Anne Dancroft tried to make herself comfortable in the heat. When she had received the telegraph message from her father two days earlier, it had taken her some time to decide to travel west to the ranch. Only the fact that there had been a note of urgency in the message had made the decision for her.

Although there had been nothing specific in it, she knew her father too well not to guess that something was wrong. He would never have sent for her like this unless something drastic had happened.

Turning her head slowly, she surveyed the other passengers in the carriage. It was only a little more than half-full. A young boy and girl were trying to peer through the dust-smeared windows but the savage glare of the sunlight meant there was little to be seen. A stout woman was seated at the very front and Anne noticed, with a slight sense of disapproval, that she was wearing a valuable necklace which was clearly visible above the expensive dress.

Such a show of extravagance was an open invitiation to any outlaws and she was quite certain that not only the stagecoaches but also trains attracted the attention of the lawless breed operating in these parts.

For an instant she glanced behind her at the man slumped in the rear seat. His hat was pulled down and she could see little of his face. He seemed to be asleep and she fervently hoped he would remain that way for the rest of her journey.

Drunken men could be a nuisance and this one looked as though he had drunk more than he should have. What he was doing on the train, and where he was going, she couldn't guess.

The conductor came along the aisle of the swaying carriage. As she handed him her ticket she asked in a low voice:

'How long before we reach Twin Forks?'

The conductor took the large watch from his waistcoat pocket and stared at it for a few moments, his lips pursed.

'Reckon it'll be dark by the time we get there, miss. You got anyone waitin' for you at the depot?'

'Yes. My father should be there.'

He nodded. 'Reckon you should be all right then. Twin Forks ain't a healthy place for a woman out at night.'

'Thank you.' Anne settled back in her seat.

Moving away, the conductor prodded the man in the back seat. The man mumbled something under his breath, glanced up and dug into his vest-pocket, producing a ticket. He handed it to the other without a word. Then he took it back and resumed his former position.

The conductor seemed on the point of saying something, then thought better of it.

Ten miles along the track, where it ran out of a narrow canyon, three men sat their mounts in the shelter of a small stand of trees. Directly in front of them a large, heavy trunk had been placed across the rails.

The men had chosen this particular spot with care. Here there was a fairly steep gradient through the pass and the train would be travelling slowly, giving the engineer sufficient time to notice the obstacle and bring the train to a halt.

Seth Morgan turned in his saddle.

'You sure he's on this train, Frank?' he said harshly.

Frank Darrell nodded tersely. 'He stayed the night in Dawson Bend. Ain't no doubt about that. And talk there was he's headed for Twin Forks with a bag full o' money for the bank there.'

'And you're sure you'd recognize him?' Slim Callen asked.

Darrell grinned viciously. 'Ain't no mistakin' him.'

'All right,' Morgan cut in. 'So we all know what to do. Frank – you and me board the train and get that money. Slim, you get on the locomotive and make sure there's no trouble from the engineers.'

His two companions nodded in agreement.

'Reckon we could relieve the other passengers o' their dollar bills too,' Frank said after a brief pause. 'Mebbe even some jewellery.'

'That's all right by me,' Morgan replied. 'Just so long as we get that bag.'

Less than five minutes later they heard the whistle of the train as it entered the gradient. Morgan ran a tongue around his dry lips. He loosened the Colt in its holster, glanced sideways at the two men with him, then gave a little nod of his head.

Moments later, with a hissing of steam, the locomotive emerged from the cutting. In almost the same instant, the engineer must have noticed the trunk across the track for there was the screech of brakes being hastily applied.

The train came to a halt within two feet of the obstacle. There came a sudden shout from the enineer.

Then the trio, bandannas pulled up over the lower half of their faces, sent their mounts pounding up the slope. Slim slid swiftly from the saddle, ran for the engine and hauled himself on board, his gun lined up on the two men.

Seth and Frank split away from him and raced alongside the track. Frank reached up, grasped the handle of the carriage door and pulled it open. Within moments, he was inside, leaning out to help Seth.

They threw open the inner door and burst into the carriage, lining up their Colts on the passengers.

'Everybody sit quite still,' Seth rasped. 'That way, no one gets hurt.'

Frank gestured with his Colt towards the little man in the black coat and hat. 'There's the man we want. The money will be in that bag he's got.'

The woman at the front screamed thinly as the two outlaws advanced into the aisle. Frank reached out a hand to grab the necklace she was wearing, his lips stretched into a menacing line.

The next second two shots rang out. For a moment, Seth stared down stupidly at the blood staining his shirt. Then he fell back against the door as his legs buckled beneath him. Beside him, Frank swayed drunkenly before falling against the woman he had attempted to rob, the gun slipping from his nerveless fingers.

Sitting stiffly in her seat, Anne suddenly found it possible to turn her head and stare behind her. Her eyes went wide with shock and amazement.

The man she thought was slouching in a drunken stupor was standing there with a smoking Colt in his left hand. He stepped out into the aisle.

'Just remain where you all are,' he said in a crisp tone. 'There are three of these *hombres* on this train. I spotted them from the window. The third one is probably on the locomotive.'

He gestured towards the conductor standing open-mouthed a few feet away. 'Get a couple of men to help you put these two into the caboose.'

'Just who are you, mister?' stammered the conductor.

'The name's Rick Farnam.' The man drew his jacket

aside exposing the star on his shirt. 'I'm a federal marshal. I got word in Dawson Bend there might be a gang waitin' to bushwhack this train.'

He glanced towards the banker, sitting white-faced in his seat. 'I guess word o' that money you're carryin' must've travelled fast.'

Before anyone else could speak, he moved back a little way, opened the carriage door and glanced out. A few heads showed in the windows of the second carriage but there was no sign of the third outlaw.

A second later, he jumped down beside the track and edged cautiously in the direction of the locomotive. Whoever the third man was, he hoped the outlaw figured those shots had been fired by his companions.

Drifting slowly along the track, he drew level with the locomotive and risked a quick glance at the footplate. The two engineers stood on the far side, their hands raised. The third outlaw was only a foot away, his back to Rick.

For a moment, he debated whether to put a bullet into the outlaw's back, then decided against it. Even with a slug in him, the man could loose off a shot and kill one of the engineers. Besides, he wanted to take this one alive if possible.

Almost without thinking, he lashed out with his right hand, grabbed the other by the ankle, and pulled hard. With a startled yell, the man fell sideways, completely off balance. His head hit the edge of the firebox, the gun in his hand going off as his finger tightened reflexively on the trigger.

There was a faint whine as the lead ricocheted off the cab and went whining into the distance.

With a savage heave, Rick pulled the outlaw from the cab, sending him sprawling on to the side of the track. Before the other could recover, Rick stamped hard on the man's arm. With a harsh yell of agony, the outlaw released his hold on the Colt.

'All right,' Rick said, levelling his own weapon on the other. 'I reckon this is the end o' the line for you. And don't expect any help from your two companions. They're both dead. But you're goin' to stand trial in Twin Forks.'

'You won't get any judge and jury to convict me,' the other growled.

'We'll see about that. Now get on your feet.'

Ten minutes later, with Slim Callen securely tied up beside the bodies of Seth Morgan and Frank Darrell, Rick and the two engineers had hauled the log off the track and the train was under way again.

Rick went into the caboose. He leaned easily against the swaying side and stared down at Callen.

'You made a big mistake holdin' up this train,' he said at last. 'You talked too much in Dawson Bend and back in Dodge City. I figgered you couldn't resist goin' for all that money Jepson was carryin' with him.'

A scowl creased Callen's swarthy features.

'Reckon you made the big mistake, mister. Seth had some mighty important people as *amigos* in this part o' the territory. Your life ain't worth a plugged nickel now he's dead.'

'Whether it is or not, reckon you won't be around to see it,' Rick replied tautly. 'My guess is you'll be swingin' on the end of a rope.'

'Don't bet on it,' grunted the other. There was a

strange glint in the close-set eyes which Rick didn't like. He seemed too sure of himself, as if he knew something which Rick didn't.

It was dark by the time the train steamed into Twin Forks. As he stepped down on to the platform, prodding his prisoner in front of him, Rick glanced about him. He noticed that only two other passengers had alighted from the train. Jepson, the banker, and the girl he had noticed back at Dawson Bend.

She was standing uncertainly in the middle of the platform, looking about her, an anxious expression on her face.

Thrusting Callen forward, the man's hands still tied behind his back, Rick moved towards the girl.

'You waitin' for someone, miss?' he asked.

'My father,' she answered, casting a wary look at Callen. 'He was supposed to meet me here.'

At that moment, the train conductor came hurrying towards them.

'What am I supposed to do with those two dead men? I can hold up the train for ten minutes but not much longer.'

Rick inclined his head in the direction of the office a short distance away.

'See if you can rouse anybody in there. Get them to send a message to the sheriff.'

The conductor hesitated for a moment, then, noticing the expression in Rick's eyes, did as he was told. He disappeared into the office and emerged a couple of minutes later with a white-whiskered oldster beside him. Gesturing towards the caboose, he spoke for a few moments and then the oldster hurried off into the darkness.

'He'll bring Sheriff Corder right away,' the conductor said when he came back.

Rick nodded. He made to speak to the girl again, then stopped. There was the sound of horses off in the distance beyond the depot. A few moments later a tall man came in sight, glancing up and down the platform. Seeing the girl, he hurried forward.

'Sorry I'm late, Anne,' he said. 'I got a visit from Ed Jordan an hour ago.' He threw a swift, enquiring glance in Rick's direction, then stepped back as he noticed the gun in Rick's hand.

Before Rick could speak, Anne said quickly:

'The train was held up not far from Dawson Bend. Three outlaws boarded it and tried to take money from the new bank manager. This is Federal Marshal Farnam. He shot two of the men, the sheriff's been sent for and—'

She broke off as her father said sharply:

'I know this man you've got, Marshal. He's Slim Callen. A no-good killer who rides with Morgan and Darrell.'

'He won't be ridin' with 'em any more,' Rick said. 'They're both lyin' in the caboose yonder. I'm takin' this one in so that the sheriff can lock him up until there's a trial.'

He noticed the gust of expression that flashed across the tall man's face. He seemed on the point of saying something, then changed his mind. Instead, he held out his hand.

'I'm Clint Dancroft. I own the Lazy W ranch some

seven miles out o' town.'

His voice took on a sober note. 'Watch your back in Twin Forks, Marshal. And above all, don't trust Corder.'

'The sheriff?'

'That's right. There ain't no proof but there are rumours he's in cahoots with some o' the lawless bunch in these parts.'

'Thanks for the warnin'. I'll keep an eye on him while I'm here.'

Five minutes later, the clerk came back. There was a short, stout figure behind him. The latter came forward, his small eyes taking in everything.

'I heard the train was held up just west o' Dawson Bend,' he said. 'Reckon I—' He broke off sharply as his glance fell on the man standing beside Rick. 'This one o' those critters?' There was an odd edge to his voice which Rick noticed at once. He felt certain that Corder had instantly recognized the outlaw. There had also been a knowing look which had passed between the two men.

'I took this one alive,' Rick said tersely. 'Figgered he might be able to answer a few questions. The other two are in the caboose.'

'Dead?'

'Weren't nothin' else I could do. There are plenty o' witnesses on this train who'll testify as to what happened, if you want to question 'em.'

'I ain't doubtin' your actions, Marshal.' Corder spoke hastily. 'That won't be necessary. I'll have the bodies taken along to the morgue.'

'Meanwhile, you'd better get this one locked up. Then I'll find myself a bed for the night.'

'Are there any questions you'd like me to answer?' Anne Dancroft asked.

Rick shook his head. 'Nothin' at the moment, miss.' He paused, then added: 'If there are any, where can I find you?'

'She'll be at the Lazy W ranch,' her father put in. 'You're welcome there at any time, Marshal.'

'Thanks. I'll remember that.' Rick waited until they had gone and the sound of hoofbeats outside the depot had died away. Then he turned to Corder. 'I assume there's a hotel in town, Sheriff?'

'Sure thing, Marshal. I'll take you there myself. Bring your prisoner and I'll find a cell for him.'

Inside the sheriff's office, Rick found two men, evidently Corder's deputies. While one of them took Callen through to the jail at the rear, Corder sent the other for the undertaker, giving him instructions to have the two bodies taken to the morgue and then let the train go on its way.

Corder seated himself behind the desk, leaned forward and lit a smoke from the lamp. Then he glanced up, a curious expression in his eyes.

'What happened on that train, Marshal?' he asked, leaning back. 'It ain't often we get any trouble like that in this part o' the territory.'

Rick shrugged. 'Like I said, there were three o' the critters. We'd already been given word that somebody might make a try for that money. That's why I was on the train.'

'Did you have to kill those other two?'

'Weren't no other way. They had their guns trained on the passengers and from the look o' those *hombres*, they wouldn't hesitate to kill anyone who resisted.'

'Pity. If this one won't talk, we might have got somethin' from them.'

Rick pulled out the other chair from under the desk and lowered himself into it. Sharply, he said:

'Somehow, I get the notion you recognized that man I brought in. Mebbe you got a Wanted picture of him.'

There was a momentary hesitation on Corder's part, then he shook his head.

'Ain't never seen him before, Marshal. And I'm certain I've got no Wanted poster for him.'

'Then I guess it might be best if you was to take a look at the other two in the mornin'. Could be you'll know them. They sure knew which train Jepson was takin'.'

'I'll do that.' Corder blew a cloud of smoke into the air. He seemed oddly ill at ease. He thrust himself to his feet.

'I'll take you over to the hotel,' he said harshly. 'Guess you could do with somethin' to eat and a night's sleep.'

Rick nodded and followed the other outside. The hotel was a tall, two-storey building on the opposite side of the street. In the lobby he found the night clerk half-asleep in the chair behind the desk.

Corder banged loudly on the desk with his fist. The clerk jerked himself to his feet, gave the sheriff a brief nod of recognition, then swung his gaze to Rick. His eyes widened slightly as he caught sight of the star on the other's shirt.

'This is Federal Marshal Farnam,' Corder said briskly. 'He wants a room and somethin' to eat.'

'Sure thing, Sheriff.' The clerk turned quickly and took a key from the wooden rack on the wall. 'How long are you stayin' in town, Marshal?'

'That depends on how long it takes to finish my business here,' Rick replied quietly. 'Could be a couple o' days, could be longer.'

Corder glanced up quickly at this.

'I figgered your job was finished, once you got that gang of outlaws' he said.

Rick's lips twisted into a tight smile.

'Not quite, Sheriff. There are a few loose ends I still have to tie up.'

Corder considered that for a moment, then shrugged.

'Well, if I can be of any help, just let me know.'

Rick waited until the sheriff had gone. Then he turned back to the clerk.

'You reckon you can rustle me up somethin' to eat?'

'Sure, Marshal. I'll see that it's ready for you in ten minutes. Just go through into the dining-room yonder.' He pointed to a short passage. Bringing a lamp from behind the desk, he followed him and placed the lamp on one of the tables.

A while later, a heaped plate of bacon, eggs and beans was placed in front of him. While he ate Rick motioned the clerk to sit opposite him. The man looked the kind eager to talk and probably knew everything that went on around Twin Forks.

Rick glanced up from his plate.

'I heard the name Ed Jordan mentioned,' he said. 'Do you know anything about him?'

'Jordan? Reckon he's the biggest man around these parts. Owns most o' the town, all three saloons. He ain't the type o' man to cross, believe me.' The clerk paused and cocked an eyebrow. 'He ain't the one you're checkin' on, is he?'

Rick pushed his empty plate away and rolled a smoke.

'Just interested, that's all,' he replied nonchalantly. He lit the cigarette and drew deeply on it. 'I also hear there's a big party o' Sioux in this area. You have any trouble with 'em?'

'Not much. Did have some a few years back when the railroad was bein' built. They didn't like it crossin' their land or the railroad men slaughterin' their buffalo but the army moved in and made a pact with their chief. Now they keep themselves to themselves. Clint Dancroft seems to get on well with 'em but I can't say the same for Jordan.'

'Why not?' Rick finished his coffee and stubbed out the cigarette.

'Couldn't say for sure. Claims they're rustlin' his beef but my guess is he's got some other reason. Talk is he's in with some big business men from back East and they want to build a line from the railroad to the north o' town. He's got a big stockyard there nearly finished and aims to ship his cattle east from here.'

'Wouldn't that be a good thing for the town?'

'Not the way Jordan aims to do it. Only his cattle will be shipped out. The rest o' the smaller ranchers won't have a say in it. They'll either have to sell out to him or drive their herds more'n two hundred miles across bad country to market.'

'Guess that answers some o' my questions,' Rick said tautly. He pushed back his chair and got to his feet. 'Thanks for the grub. Guess I'll get myself some sleep.'

He went up to his room on the top floor and locked

the door behind him. Outside his window the wide street was clearly visible. Music came from the saloons and there were several horses tethered to the hitching rail on the opposite side.

Over to his left, he noticed there was still a light showing in the window of the sheriff's office. He placed his gunbelt on the small bedside table within easy reach of his hand, took off his jacket and stretched himself out on the bed.

There was evidently a lot going on around Twin Forks about which he knew nothing. Clint Dancroft had clearly not been happy when he had mentioned Jordan's name to his daughter. As for the sheriff, he was obviously lying when he claimed he had no knowledge of the outlaw he had brought in.

Some instinct, born of long years of experience, told him that Callen wouldn't stay in jail for long. Whether he was tied in with Jordan in any way was problematical. If he was, then Jordan would make sure the man never came to trial.

Corder hadn't been too pleased when he'd said he intended staying in town for some time. While he was there, any attempt to free the outlaw would prove extremely difficult. The sheriff would have to be sure he was out of town before he made his play. Wondering whether the two deputies were to be trusted, he fell asleep.

The next morning, Rick made his way over to the sheriff's office. He found Corder seated behind his desk. There was another man there seated in the chair in front of him. Both men lifted their heads sharply as Rick walked in.

He instantly took in the expensive clothes the big man wore and the diamond tie-pin above the velvet waistcoat. There had been a scowl of ill-concealed anger on the man's face but this was wiped away instantly as he saw the star on Rick's shirt.

Corder scraped back his chair. For a moment, he seemed confused as if taken off balance by Rick's sudden appearance. Then he controlled himself with an effort.

'This is Mr Jordan, Marshal,' he said tightly. Even though there was, as yet, little heat in the air, he was sweating profusely.

Jordan rose lazily from the chair and held out his hand.

'I heard you were in town, Marshal.' His narrowed eyes bored into Rick. 'I was just sayin' to the sheriff, it's a long time since we had any trouble like this in the territory. Even though that hold-up happened back east of here, it still reflects badly on the town.'

Shaking hands, Rink said thinly:

'You got any interest in this coyote I brought in last night, Mr Jordan?'

The other's eyes narrowed to mere slits at Rick's words. Then he forced himself to relax.

'Only insofar as I want to see justice done. I have suggested to the sheriff that it might be better if this outlaw was taken to Dawson Bend to stand trial there.' He glanced across the desk at Corder. 'I'm sure you could spare one o' your deputies to make sure he gets there.'

'Sure thing.' Corder nodded enthusiastically. 'That won't be any trouble at all.'

'That critter stays here,' Rick said brusquely. 'There are some questions I intend to ask him.'

Watching the reactions of the two men, Rick knew that this was the last thing they wanted.

'Now see here, Marshal,' Jordan said. His voice was like an iron bar. 'As far as I'm concerned, that man is now Sheriff Corder's prisoner so long as he's locked up in this jail. You're a stranger here. You know nothin' of this town.'

Rick pursed his lips into a hard line. He meant to make a sharp retort but choked it down. Instead, he said:

'I hear you intend to run a line from the railroad to your stockade so you can ship 'em direct to the East.'

'Guess you heard right,' Jordan affirmed. He was still puzzled and angry at Rick's attitude. 'Far as I know, there ain't no law against that.'

'There might be if you mean to run that line through Indian territory.'

Jordan gave a derisive snort.

'There'll be no trouble from them. The army put them in their place and if necessary, I reckon I can call in the soldiers again.'

'You're willin' to risk a full-scale Indian war just to get what you want?'

Jordan's lips twisted into a faint sneer.

'I always get what I want, Marshal.'

Throwing a quick, meaningful glance at the sheriff, Jordan turned and brushed past Rick, turned on to the boardwalk and headed towards the Last Trail saloon.

Rick turned to follow, then paused in the doorway as Corder said quietly:

'If you want my advice, Marshal, I'd ride outa town today. Head back to where you came from. Jordan ain't a man to cross. He's got most o' the town in the palm of his hand and there are some who won't take kindly to you killin' those two outlaws.'

'Now just what does that mean, Sheriff?' Rick's tone held an ominous note which Corder recognized at once.

'I'm just givin' you fair warnin', that's all. Men have tried to stand up to Jordan in the past and—'

'And some kind of accident has happened. Well, I guess I can take care of myself. I've seen places like this before, met men like Jordan before.'

Before stopping out on to the boardwalk, he added: 'You can let Jordan know that when I come to a place that wants me out in a goddamn hurry, that's when I decide to stay.'

CHAPTER TWO

VENGEANCE TRAIL

Twin Forks was quiet and the street almost deserted when Rick made his way towards the livery stables he had noticed earlier at the end of town.

There was no one in sight when he entered but a few moments later, a man sidled in from the back. He eyed Rick speculatively.

'You lookin' for a mount, mister?' he asked.

'I came in on the train yesterday,' Rick explained. 'Reckon I'll need a good horse if you've got one.'

'Sure. I—' The man broke off sharply as he noticed the star. 'Say, you're the marshal who shot them two polecats who held up the train, ain't you?'

'That's right.' Mick gave a short nod.

'I guess I can let you have this stallion.' The man indicated a large black horse in the end stall. 'He's a mean critter but you look like the kind of man who can tame him.'

'He'll do. I'd also like a saddle and bridle.'

The man went into the back, then returned and stood

watching as Rick threw the saddle on to the mount and tightened the cinch under the animal's belly.

After paying the man, Rick climbed into the saddle and rode out. It was only a little after high noon and the heat which lay like a smothering blanket on the dusty street was blistering and oppressive.

Most of the townsfolk were indoors, waiting for the coolness which came with the approach of evening. He spotted only a couple of old-timers seated in rickety cane chairs on the boardwalk, seeking a little shade from the awnings over the shop doors.

Discreet inquiries of the hotel clerk had given him the directions to the Lazy W ranch. He had decided it was time to obtain a little more information as to what was happening around town and, at the moment, he could think of no better man to give it to him than Clint Dancroft.

It was clear from what he had overheard at the train depot that Jordan was somehow connected with Dancroft but, to Rick's way of thinking, it was not an amicable arrangement.

As he rode along the single street, he knew there were eyes watching all the way. By now, his arrival in Twin Forks would be known to virtually everyone, as would news of the hold-up further along the track.

A hundred yards beyond the end of the street, the trail forked. He swung his mount and took the left trail, following a steep downgrade. Ahead of him, the track ran through a steep-walled canyon, hemmed in by long overhangs.

He threw a quick glance behind him and satisfied himself that he hadn't been followed from town. Yet, somehow, he had the feeling of trouble ready to break. It was a sensation he had experienced many times in the past and one he had learned never to ignore. Gently, he eased the Colt in its holster and gigged the stallion forward.

Nevertheless the shot, when it came, took him momentarily off guard. The slug hummed within an inch of his head and whined off the rocks to his left as he slid swiftly from the saddle. He crouched down swiftly and let his glance sweep along the ravine wall.

The faint puff of rifle smoke was still just visible at the top of the ravine almost level with him. The man was lying behind two tightly packed boulders and had fired through the narrow cleft between them.

Rick instantly recognized that while this meant the bushwhacker was well shielded againt any return fire, it strictly limited the arc through which he could swing the rifle. He got his feet under him and loosed off a snap shot at the other. Then, bending almost double, he thrust himself forward, running in a zigzag course across the canyon floor.

A second shot came but the slug struck the ground almost a yard away. The next moment, he was lying against a jumble of rocks almost immediately below where the gunman was hidden.

'You won't shoot me down without any warnin' like you did my brother,' yelled a hoarse voice. 'Seth never had a fair chance.'

Seth? Rick tightened his lips. So that was the reason for this ambush. Seth Morgan's brother! At least that explained why Callen had been so certain he was heading into big trouble coming to Twin Forks.

He glanced swiftly about him, trying to find some cover from where be could get a shot at the man above him. There were a few scattered boulders but even if he managed to reach one, the gunhawk had picked an excellent spot. Crouched behind those rocks, it would be virtually impossible to hit him.

There was just one chance. A slim one but it might work.

'Your brother was nothin' more than a lowdown killer,' he shouted loudly. 'He deserved all he got. Just like those other two gunslingers.'

A pause then, 'It was you who made the mistake, lawman. Now I aim to make you pay. There ain't no way you can get outa here alive.'

Rick nodded to himself, satisfied. The sound had come from above him, a little way to his left. Clearly, the gunman was so sure of himself he hadn't moved his position.

He tensed himself, hefted the Colt in his left hand, sucked in a deep breath, then swung himself away from the rocks. Swiftly, he straightened up, aimed at the narrow gap between the twin rocks to hit the inner surface of the further boulder.

Three shots rang out in rapid succession.

Scarcely had the echoes died away than he picked out a shuddering gasp from the killer. No return fire came from above. Letting out his pent-up breath in a long exhalation, Rick guessed that his stratagem had worked. He reckoned that at least one, possibly two, of those slugs had ricocheted off the rock and found their mark.

When there was no further sign of any movement, he returned to his mount, swung up into the saddle and let the horse have its head as he followed the trail and then swung back towards the steep climb to the canyon rim.

Five minutes later, he spotted the body lying behind the rocks. He slid from the saddle and went forward warily, his finger tight on the trigger of the Colt, ready for any sudden movement. But there was none.

He turned the man over with his foot and saw where the deflected slugs had struck the other in the temple, just above his right eye.

Back in town, Jordan had seen Rick ride out. Now he went back to Corder's office where he found the sheriff rifling through a sheaf of Wanted posters.

Corder glanced up a trifle guiltily, made to stuff the posters back into his drawer, then left them where they were when he saw who it was.

'Just figgered I'd get rid o' some o' these' he said. 'In case that marshal wants to look through 'em. He might find some o' your boys among them.'

'Good thinkin',' Jordan nodded. He sat down heavily in the other chair. 'It's this marshal I want to talk to you about. He's goin' to cause trouble around here, big trouble, if we don't stop him.'

Corder sat back. 'How d'you figger on doin' that? It ain't easy to get rid of a federal marshal. Somebody back East is sure to know where he is and we might got even bigger trouble.'

Jordan pulled out a cigar from his vest pocket. He bit off the end and spat it on to the floor before applying a match to the other end.

'I reckon there are ways. I've got some men comin' into Twin Forks in the next couple o' days to start layin' that track from the railroad.'

Corder digested that information for a moment, eyes narrowing.

'You know what that'll do where those Sioux are concerned.'

Jordan's smile was a menacing twist of his lips. He blew a cloud of smoke into the air.

'They won't like it. That's what I'm bankin' on. But if we get word to their chief that Dancroft is behind it . . .' He deliberately left the remainder of his sentence unsaid.

'You think he'll believe you. From what I've heard, these Indians ain't very friendly towards you.'

Jordan's smile broadened slightly. 'Oh, I ain't goin' to tell 'em. You are.'

Corder's face twisted.

'What makes you think they'll even listen to me?'

'Why shouldn't they? You're the elected law in this town. If Dancroft steps outa line, it's your duty to inform the Sioux. They got rights around here just like everyone else.'

Corder noticed the expression of sardonic amusement on the other's face but said nothing. So far, the Sioux had remained peaceful. But if Jordan went ahead with his plan, he could foresee a full-scale war breaking out. For a moment, he considered arguing, then thought better of it.

There was a little thought at the back of his mind of intimating this to the marshal. But it would have to be done without Jordan getting an inkling of it.

'If you get those Indians all fired up, there'll be a wholesale slaughter. You wouldn't be able to atop that. Besides, ain't you overlooked one thing?'

'Oh, what's that?'

'The Sioux ain't stupid. Even if you turn 'em against Dancroft, they'll know it ain't him who's runnin' a line across their land. They'll kill those railroad men you bring in and you'll never get that line through to the other side o' town.'

Jordan turned slightly and leaned forward, placing his elbows on the desk. He thrust his face close up to Corder's.

'You know the reason why you're just a low-paid sheriff in a one-horse frontier town and I own virtually all of it?'

Corder flushed but said nothing.

'It's because I work out everythin' down to the last detail and I've got the guts to get everythin' I want.'

He paused to let that remark sink in. Then he continued: 'I got a friend at Fort Denson who owes me a favour. It'll take me half a day to get word to him that Dancroft is killin' Indians and I need some troops to protect my men. That'll be the end of Dancroft. If the army won't arrest him for violatin' the Indian laws, then I reckon the Sioux will take care of him.'

'The Sioux have lived in peace with ranchers like Dancroft for years,' Corder protested, believing he had found a flaw in the other's argument. 'You'd need one helluva lot to convince that federal marshal that any o' Dancroft's men have killed any o' them.'

Jordan pulled his thick lips back flat across his teeth.

'That ain't goin' to be too difficult. Just leave that to me. I've already put that in hand. In the meantime, I want you to ride out to Fort Denson and see Captain Ford. Give him this note.' He passed a folded sheet of paper across the desk. 'And you'll also tell him of your own suspicions.'

Jordan pushed back his chair, stood looking down menacingly at the other. 'You'll do exactly as I say, otherwise there'll be a new sheriff in Twin Forks, one who'll do what he's told without question.'

The threat behind the remark was clear enough. Corder gave a brief nod.

'I'll leave the place to my deputies and ride out to the fort. I only hope you know what you're doin'. If this plan o' yours gets out o' hand, there won't be much o' Twin Forks left.'

The two men had been riding through thickly tangled slopes during most of the morning and now, with the sun climbing towards its zenith, they came out of the pines into flat, open country that stretched away to a limitless horizon.

Acting on Jordan's orders, Pete Rodriguez and Jed Wesson now headed their mounts towards the Indian territory. Eyes narrowed to mere slits against the vicious sunglare, Wesson muttered:

'You're sure we'll find any Sioux braves out this way?'

His companion allowed himself a slow, lazy nod.

'There's buffalo yonder, not more'n three miles away on the flats. They'll be there like the boss says.'

'Just so long as we don't run into a big party of 'em, or we may end up dead.'

Neither man had any compunction against shooting down men in cold blood. Ed Jordan chose his men well, men bred to killing and violence. To hired gunslingers like Wesson and Rodriguez, it was all part of a day's work.

Ten minutes' riding through mesquite and thick brush brought them to the border of the rich grasslands. It was here that the buffalo roamed in their thousands, providing the Sioux with their staple diet. Topping a low rise, the two men came in sight of a herd less than a mile away.

It wasn't a big group. Rodriguez reckoned there were about 200 head, grazing on the lush grass. Slowly, the two men edged their mounts towards the east, taking care to remain downwind of the animals.

Lifting himself high in the saddle, Wesson scanned the ground nearby. He eventually shook his head, an expression of disappointment on his hard features.

'Don't see any sign of Indians around,' he muttered. 'Reckon they're—' He broke off abruptly as his companion reached out and grabbed his arm, pointing.

About half a mile to their right a low, rocky escarpment thrust out of the fiat prairie. Halfway along it, a plume of white smoke climbed lazily into the still air.

'Looks like we found what we're lookin' for,' Rodriguez said with a vicious grin on his swarthy features. Very slowly, he slid his Winchester from the scabbard near his waist. Wesson did likewise before gigging his mount forward at a slow pace.

Before they reached the small hollow they made out the trio of Palomino ponies standing against the rock-face. A couple of dead buffalo lay close by. The three Sioux were seated around the fire, talking together in low tones. Each had a rifle lying close by but it was evident from their relaxed attitudes that they were expecting no danger.

Ever since the building of the railroad when the railroaders had taking to slaughtering the buffalo, the army scouts had forged an uneasy pact with the Indians.

Now, with the railroad gangs gone, the Sioux had the right to hunt these animals as they had for centuries.

Even when Wesson and Rodriguez rode into full view, there was only curiosity on the faces of the three braves.

One of them waved a hand in greeting and pointed towards the fire, inviting them to sit wth them.

'Friendly critters, ain't they,' Wesson muttered sardonically.

'Sure are,' Rodriguez agreed. 'Reckon they figure we're Dancroft's men.'

Hefting the rifle in one hand, he levelled it squarely on the nearest Sioux's chest and pulled the trigger. In almost the same instant, Wesson shot the second. He grinned viciously as he saw the other fall back into the dust.

The third brave, a look of startled astonishment on his lean features, had half-risen to his feet, one hand going for the rifle beside him, when Rodrigues shot him. All three died without a single cry.

Wesson slid from the saddle.

'Get those ponies before they stampede,' he said sharply. 'We've got to get these bodies on to Dancroft's land before any more o' the tribe comes lookin' for 'em.'

Rodriguez ran forward, caught at the short ropes and brought the ponies across, cursing savagely under his breath as the animals fought against him.

Between them, the two men lifted the dead Indians across the backs of their ponies. It wasn't easy. The animals were skittish, scenting blood.

Rodriguez looped two of the ropes around his pommel and swung back into the saddle. Wesson kicked sand on to the fire, extinguishing it. He went back to his own mount and tied the third rope around his saddlehorn. A moment later they set off towards the trees on the skyline, leading the ponies and their inert burdens behind them. Both men kept a sharp lookout for any other Sioux in the vicinity.

Fortunately, the three they had killed appeared to be a small hunting party and they saw no one. As they reached the trees, the trail became narrower and they were forced to ride more slowly.

Even here, they were not safe from trouble. Two miles further on they would cross into Dancroft's land and there was the possibility some of his hired hands might be riding the rim of the ranchland. Jordan had impressed on them both the need for absolute caution.

All of this had to be done without anyone spotting them. Once they had these three bodies placed within the perimeter of Dancroft's spread and got away without being seen, everything would point to their having been killed there, shot by him or his men. There wouldn't be a jury in the entire territory that wouldn't convict him of ordering the killing of unarmed Sioux.

The thought appealed to Rodriguez's sadistic sense of perverted justice. Since Jordan had hired him a couple of years earlier, his one worry was that the Sioux might take it into their heads to launch an attack against Jordan's spread.

He knew that his boss had no liking for the Indians and had shown his dislike openly. Fast as he was with a gun, and a man driven by killing lust, he didn't like the idea of a couple of thousand Indians on the warpath. This way, Jordan had almost certainly taken out two of his enemies at a single stroke.

His thoughts stopped at a sudden hissed warning

from his companion. Jerking his head round, he saw that the other had abruptly reined up his mount and was pointing to their right.

'A rider yonder,' Wesson muttered in a low voice. 'Could be one o' Dancroft's men.'

Rodriguez sat quite still, cursing himself for allowing his thoughts to wander. Judging from the sound, there was only one man moving parallel to them and he guessed the other was at least half a mile away.

His right hand dropped towards his rifle, stopped as Wesson hissed:

'Don't be a fool! We can't afford a gunfight here.'

'Can you make him out?'

Wesson shook his head. 'He's on the other trail. With luck, he'll keep on ridin'. If it is one o' Dancroft's men, we could testify he was in the vicinity when these were shot.'

Gradually, the sound of hoofbeats faded into the distance. The two men waited for several minutes after the silence returned, then edged their horses forward. They came out of the timber a little while later and in front of them made out the long fence which marked the boundary of the Lazy W ranch.

Here they waited until they were certain there was no one around. A small creek meandered down from the slopes and across the rich prairie.

'Reckon I can see why Jordan wants to get his hands on this land,' Rodriguez remarked as they approached the fence. 'Must have some o' the best grazin' in the territory.'

Wesson uttered a harsh laugh as he dismounted.

'Once we park these bodies, reckon it won't be long before he gets it.'

The Mexican stepped down beside him and examined the fence with a critical eye.

'How do you figger we should go about this?' he asked.

'We bust the fence down,' the other muttered. 'Reckon that's what these braves would do if they attacked the spread.'

Rodriguez thought that over for a minute, then shook his head.

'We have to be careful about this, *amigo.* It has to look like these Indians came here peaceable and were shot down in cold blood. If it was to look like they smashed down the fence, Dancroft could claim they was rustlin' his cattle and his men would have every right to shoot 'em.'

He jerked a thumb in the direction of the creek. 'We take 'em in that way.'

Where the water ran under the wire, only two strands crossed it and there was a space high and wide enough for a man to crawl through. Using the creek as a means of entry on to the land also had the advantage that the rushing water would remove any footprints.

It took them the best part of half an hour to drag the three bodies through the gap. Once this was done, they left them along the bank of the creek. The three Palominos they turned loose, knowing the animals would somehow find their way back to the Sioux camp. It would not be long before the Indians came looking for the three braves.

The Lazy W ranch house was a typical frontier building with a long veranda in front and a wide courtyard.

There were three barns standing to one side and a bunkhouse at the rear.

Several horses were tethered at the front of the house as Rick rode towards it. He had expected to find men watching the trail but had seen no one. Either Dancroft was confident that no move would be made against him in the short term, or his men were far better at keeping themselves out of sight than Rick had imagined.

The door opened as he stepped down from the saddle and the girl he had met on the train stood there, eyeing him with a frank, open gaze.

'I see you accepted my father's offer to visit us, Marshal,' she said in a low, husky voice.

'Figured it might be wise to have a talk with him, miss,' Rick replied. 'Seems to me there's a lot o' trouble brewin' around Twin Forks and I'd like to know what's behind it all.'

'I can tell you that in two words,' Anne replied. 'Ed Jordan.'

Rick gave a brief smile.

'Somehow, I figgered that name would come up.'

'He's got the sheriff, Jeb Dressler, the lawyer, and—'

'It's all right, Anne.' The voice broke in from immediately behind the girl and her father came out on to the veranda. He looked down at Rick. 'I guess you'd like somethin' to drink, Marshal. It's a long, dusty ride from town. Bring us some coffee, Anne. We'll talk out here.'

As Anne went inside, he motioned to one of the chairs near the porch. 'Sit down, Marshal. I'm mighty glad you came. At the moment, the only law around Twin Forks is Jordan's. The rest of us smaller ranchers ain't got no one else to complain to. Like my daughter said, even the lawyer is in Jordan's pocket.'

Rick tightened his lips. He had seen all of this before, not once, but many times. An unscrupulous, avaricious man setting himself up over everyone else. Those ranchers who wouldn't sell out at a fraction of what their spreads were worth would be either driven out or killed.

'Reckon there's only one way to fight men like Jordan,' he said at last. 'You have to unite and take the fight to him. Otherwise, he'll pick you off one by one. That's the way these *hombres* operate.'

'Trouble is, all of our men are just hired hands, useful for mendin' fences and ridin' herd. But they ain't gunslingers like those that Jordan has on his payroll.'

At that moment, Anne came out with the coffee. As she handed the mug to him, she said in a worried tone:

'What my father hasn't told you is that the bank is threatening to foreclose on any outstanding loans. It's never happened this way before. They never call in any bills while there's a drought like this.'

'That's true,' her father affirmed. 'But I guess the reason ain't far to seek. This new manager who came in on the train yesterday ain't wastin' any time.'

'Could be he ain't got any choice,' Rick said, grimly. 'If Jordan were to threaten to take all of his money out o' the bank and transfer it elsewhere, the bank folk back East wouldn't like that.' After an uneasy pause, he asked: 'How are you fixed as far as the drought is concerned?'

'Not as bad as several o' the others. There's still plenty o' water in the creek and—'

He broke off sharply as a lone rider swung off the trail and rode into the courtyard, dismounting before the horse had come to a standstill. The man strode quickly to the porch.

'What is it, Clyde?' Dancroft called harshly.

'A bunch o' riders headin' this way, boss,' the man answered. He wiped the beading of sweat from his forehead with the back of his hand. 'Spotted 'em about three miles back.'

'You recognize any of 'em?'

'Two of 'em. Ed Jordan and one o' Corder's deputies.'

Dancroft swung sharply on his daughter. 'Better get inside, Anne,' he said tautly. 'I've no idea what these men have in mind but Jordan's in on it.' To Rick, he added: 'Jordan came yesterday and made me an offer for the spread. When I told him to go to hell, he said it was my last chance and I'd have to take the consequences.'

Rick got to his feet. 'I'll wait inside.' he said grimly. 'I'd sure like to know what they've got in mind, but they'll clam up if they see me.'

'What about your mount?' Anne asked.

'I doubt if they'll recognize it. I only picked it up a few hours ago.'

Rick followed the girl into the house, standing just inside the doorway.

Ten minutes later, the band of men rode into the courtyard. Jordan reined up in front of Dancroft and leaned forward in the saddle.

'You aimin' to force me out with this so-called law o' yours, Jordan?' Dancroft called.

Jordan shook his head. 'These men ain't nothin' to do with me, Dancroft. I just rode out to see if you've reconsidered my offer. I met up with 'em along the trail.'

'That's right,' the deputy said. He seemed ill at ease, sitting rigidly in the saddle.

'Then why are you here?' Dancroft demanded. 'Where's Corder?'

'The sheriff ain't available at the moment. He had to ride out o' town on urgent business. I'm here in his place.'

'All right. Then state your business and then get off my land.'

The deputy swallowed hard.

'Two o' Mr Jordan's men rode into town half an hour ago,' he said. 'They claimed they'd heard gunfire at the west perimeter o' the Lazy W spread. Reckon if that's true, it's my job to investigate it.'

'I was out there an hour or so ago. There was nothin' wrong then,' Dancroft replied.

'Then you ain't got any objection to us ridin' out there and takin' a look-see.'

'Suit yourself. But I think I'll ride out with you.'

'I guess I'll come too.' Rick stepped through the open doorway. 'Seems mighty odd those two men hearin' gunfire and not goin' to take a look.'

'This has nothin' to do with you, Marshal,' Jordan butted in. 'You ain't the law in Twin Forks.'

'Then let's say I'm makin' it my business.' There was an ominous ring to Rick's tone.

CHAPTER THREE

TWISTED JUSTICE

The three bodies of the murdered Sioux were discovered half an hour later beside the creek. Jordan deliberately kept himself in the background as the deputy and his posse bent to examine them.

Eventually the deputy straightened up, his features set in grim lines.

'All of 'em shot at close range,' he said harshly. 'No doubt about that. And from the looks of 'em, I'd say they were shot less than a couple of hours ago. The blood's still fresh.' He swung his gaze towards Dancroft. 'You say none o' your men have been here for some time except you.'

'That's right.' Dancroft spoke through his teeth. 'And those Indians weren't there when I left.'

'But you ain't denyin' they're on your land,' Jordan put in. 'And as far as I can see, your fence is still intact.' He turned to address the deputy. 'Any of them have any weapons?'

After a brief examination the lawman shook his head.

'Only a huntin'-knife each. Apart from that, they're unarmed.'

'Then whoever did it shot 'em down in cold blood.' Jordan let nothing show through on his face. Inwardly, he was congratulating himself on the success of his plan and the efficient way Rodriguez and Wesson had carried it out. So far, everything was going perfectly.

'Guess that goes without sayin',' the deputy agreed. 'Reckon you'd better ride back into town with me, Mr Dancroft. There are some questions Sheriff Corder will want to ask once he gets back.'

Dancroft's jaw hardened.

'You accusin' me of killin' these braves?'

'I'm sayin' that all of the evidence points to you as the killer. And once the Sioux get wind o' this, there'll be big trouble and you'll be in the middle of it.'

'One thing you seem to have overlooked, Deputy.' Rick spoke for the frist time.

'Oh, and what's that?'

Rick pointed. 'Take a good look at these three bodies. One of 'em is only two or three feet from the fence and from the way he's lyin', he must have been facin' that way when he was shot.'

'So he was tryin' to escape,' Jordan interrupted.

'Then if that were so, he'd have been shot in the back. All three were obviously shot from the front.'

'Just what are you sayin', Marshal?' Dancroft asked.

'Well, to me it sure looks as though these men were killed elsewhere and then brought here.'

'And it's just as likely he was spun round by the force

o' that slug,' Jordan retorted. 'The way he's lyin' don't prove a damned thing.'

The deputy gave a brief nod. 'You're right, Mr Jordan. It don't.' He jerked a thumb towards Dancroft. 'I'm takin' you in. It's up to the sheriff to decide what to do with you.'

Dancroft's hand dropped towards his gun, then stopped as Rick spoke. 'Better do as he says. These men are just itchin' for an excuse to shoot you. I'll let your daughter know what's happened.'

He paused, then swung his piercing gaze to take in Jordan and the deputy. 'In the meantime, I'm goin' to start making some enquiries of my own.'

'Just keep outa this, Marshal,' Jordan snapped. 'You got no jurisdiction here in these matters.'

'That's where you're wrong, Jordan. Because I've got the suspicion that someone here is tryin' to incite the Sioux into a range war against some o' the ranchers in this territory and I'm makin' it my business.'

'Then you'd better get some proof o' that. Because I've got friends both back East and at Fort Denson and they might have somethin' to say about a jumped-up marshal pokin' his nose into things that don't concern him. Your job here finished when you stopped that hold-up and brought that outlaw into town.'

Rick knew the other was trying to rile him, make him do something foolish. With an effort, he held his anger in check. Now, more than ever, he was convinced that Dancroft had been framed, that Jordan's men had killed these Indians and planted them on the spread.

Some might claim it was sheer coincidence those two men being in the vicinity of the Lazy W spread and hearing gunfire – but where murder was concerned, Rick didn't believe in coincidence.

At the moment, however, there was little he could do to help Dancroft. He rode from the ranch with the others, the bodies of the dead Sioux over three horses, waited until they had taken the trail back into town, then returned to the ranch house.

He found Anne standing on the veranda steps watching anxiously for her father's return. When she saw no one with him, she stepped down and hurried across the courtyard towards him, grabbing at the bridle.

'What's happened?' she asked breathlessly. There was an expression of alarm on her face. 'Where's my father?'

He stepped down and led her into the house.

'We found three Sioux braves near the perimeter fence,' he told her. 'The deputy reckons your father shot them for intrudin' on to the spread.'

'But all of that's a lie,' Anne declared hotly. 'My father always got on well with the Sioux. He would never have shot any.'

'Don't you think I know that? Someone killed those Indians miles from the spread and deliberately put their bodies where we found 'em. But so far, we can't prove that.'

'So you're going to leave him in jail while Corder gets a rigged jury together and they hang him.' Her initial alarm had now turned to fear.

Rick shook his head. 'I don't aim to let that happen.'

'But what can you do?' There was a pleading note in her voice now.

'First I think I'll have a talk with the Sioux. I'm

damned certain none o' them has been on your father's land. Mebbe I can keep them under control until all o' this is sorted out. Then I'll stick around town, just to keep an eye on things. Jordan has some plan in mind and the sooner I know what it is, the better.'

'Then take care and watch your back. At the moment you seem to be the only one on our side.'

'I'll bear that in mind.' he said. 'You sure you'll be all right here on your own?'

'I'll be fine. Besides, there are plenty of the boys around. All of them are loyal to my father.'

Rick nodded and went out into the courtyard. Two minutes later he was heading for the range and the Sioux camp.

The camp was larger than Rick had expected. It was situated some fifteen miles from Twin Forks in a wide valley between rolling hills. Riding slowly, keeping his hands in sight, well away from the Colt, he swept his keen gaze over the long rows of wigwams. The men he passed eyed him with curiosity but he saw no sign of hostility. Inwardly, he was aware that all this could change if Jordan succeeded in stirring them up against the ranchers.

He had had some contact with the various tribes in the past. Some were still smarting over the wars against the white men and the depletion of the buffalo herds at the hands of the railroad gangs.

A little way inside the camp, two Sioux suddenly stepped out on to the narrow track directly in front of him. One held up his right hand. He spoke in broken English.

'Why are you here? What is it you seek?' he asked.

Bending low in the saddle, Rick said evenly:

'I come to speak with your chief. Take me to him.'

Without a further word, one of the braves turned and walked towards one of the larger wigwams, motioning him to follow.

He dismounted and waited as the other opened the flap and went inside. As he stood there, he felt a little itch between his shoulder blades, a warning tingle.

Then the brave emerged and signalled him to enter.

'Chief Shangawa will speak with you,' he said.

Ducking his head, Rick stepped inside. In the dim light, he made out the old man seated cross-legged on a thick blanket. Raising his hand in greeting, Rick stood looking down at the other.

'Sit, lawman,' Shangawa said. 'You come to see me. What is it you have to say?'

Shangawa took the long pipe lying beside him, sucked on it and blew smoke into the air before handing it to Rick.

Rick took it, drew on it, then handed it back. 'I come about three of your braves,' he said. 'They were found on Dancroft's land. All three had been shot.'

If the other felt any anger or surprise, nothing showed on his lined, impassive features.

'You say they were there stealing cattle? No Sioux would do that. We are friends of Dancroft.'

'My belief is that they were killed by Jordan's men and their bodies taken there to make it appear that Dancroft killed them. Right now, he's in jail accused of their murder.'

Shangawa pondered that for several moments.

'That I believe,' he said then. 'This man Jordan has no liking for the Sioux. He wishes to take our land, to drive us into the hills. He brings in men who hunt and kill our buffalo.'

'Then I would ask that you keep your braves under control for the time being. If I can prove that Jordan has done this, I can promise that the white man's law will punish him.'

There was a shrewd expression in Shangawa's eyes which told Rick that the Sioux chief was aware of more of what was happening than he had thought.

'Jordan is an evil man who wants all of this land for himself. He has talked with certain men like himself at the army fort. He speaks with forked tongue against my people. The lawman from Twin Forks has ridden out to the fort today, not more than four hours ago.'

Rick's head jerked up in surprise at that news.

'You're sure of this?'

'We know of all who travel the trails close to our land,' Shangawa replied solemnly.

Rick did not doubt the old chief's words. Almost certainly Corder would be acting on Jordan's orders. So why would he need the army? They were only stationed here to enforce law and order in the event of an Indian uprising.

Shangawa eyed him seriously for a few moments. Then he spoke.

'You should also know one other thing, lawman. Smoke signals have been seen in the hills in that direction.' He lifted an arm and pointed towards the west. 'There are Apache there. Not many. But there is no doubt they mean to cause big trouble. They still wish to kill the white man.'

A little finger of ice crawled along Rick's spine at these words. If there was a band of renegade Apache in the territory, Shangawa's revelation was an understatement. He had come up against these warrior bands before, had ridden past isolated ranches which had been burnt out, whole families scalped.

'Thanks for the information.' Rick got to his feet. 'I reckon the army can take care of any Apache. But I would ask that the Sioux remain at peace.'

'You have Shengawa's word.'

Night had fallen by the time Rick rode back into town. Lights showed yellowly in the windows of the saloons on either side of the street. He tethered his mount outside the hotel, went inside and ordered a meal.

As he ate, he kept an eye on the sheriff's office almost directly opposite. There was a light in the window and occasionally a shadow passed across it. Sitting there, he tried to marshal his confused thoughts into some kind of order. He had learned a lot in a single day and all of it pointed towards big trouble brewing – and in the very near future.

In the middle of it all was Ed Jordan like a spider at the centre of a web, his fingers in everything that was going on. With a crooked sheriff in charge, none of the smaller ranchers had any chance of fair treatment at the hands of the law. There was also that band of Apache. If Jordan plied them with enough whiskey and weapons, all hell would break loose.

A sudden movement across the street caught his attention. The door of the sheriff's office had opened and a figure stepped out on to the boardwalk. Even though the man's face was in shadow, silhouetted against the swath of yellow light from inside, Rick recognized him instantly. Sheriff Corder. Evidently the other had returned from Fort Denson some time earlier.

Rick got up from the table, went outside and crossed the street to where the other stood in the shadows, smoking the cigar he had just lit.

He saw Corder's expression change as he came up to him. Before Rick could speak, Corder said thinly:

'I figured you'd be on your way outa Twin Forks by now, Marshal.'

Rick smiled grimly. 'I ain't goin' nowhere while you've got Dancroft in jail on a trumped-up charge.'

Corder's thick brows drew together into a line.

'I don't see it's got anythin' to do with you,' he said defiantly. 'Accordin' to my deputy, those Sioux were found on Dancroft's spread, all unarmed and shot in the chest. Dancroft admitted bein' there only a little while before.'

'And you know as well as I do that Dancroft's got no grudge against the Sioux. Even if they had trespassed on his land, he'd never have shot 'em.'

'Guess that'll be for a jury to decide. I'm just the sheriff. He'll get a fair trial when the time comes.'

'If he ever gets to trial,' Rick grated harshly. 'I figure Jordan might like it better if somethin' was to happen to him in the meantime.'

For a moment, there was a flicker of emotion at the back of the other's close-set eyes. Rick tried to gauge what it was – anger, maybe, or perhaps fear.

'You're talkin' outa turn now, Marshal. So long as he's locked up in the jail, he's safe and in my custody.'

Rick switched the subject.

'I understand from your deputy that two o' Jordan's men came into town and reported hearin' gunfire near Dancroft's spread. Mind tellin' me who they were?'

He saw Corder stiffen abruptly at that question. Summoning up his courage, the other remarked:

'I don't have to give you that information. This don't concern you.'

'No?' Rick's tone hardened. 'Either you give me their names and where I can find 'em, or—'

'Or what?' Corder blustered.

'Or I send a telegraph message to Denver and by this time tomorrow there'll be half a dozen federal marshals here and they'll take this town apart. Could be that at the end of it, there'll be a new sheriff in Twin Forks.'

'You can't do that.' Now there was a definite look of apprehension on the other's face.

'I can – and I will.'

Corder seemed to shrink visibly at the note of menace in Rick's voice.

'Very well, I'll tell you,' he said, weakly. 'But it ain't goin' to help you. They were Pete Rodriguez and Jed Wesson.'

'Jordan's men?'

'That's right. But if you're tryin' to pin anythin' on them, you're ridin' the wrong trail. They had every right to be where they were at that time. Jordan's land borders on Dancroft's at that western perimeter.'

'And where do I find 'em?'

Corder shrugged. 'Reckon they'll both be in the

Prairie saloon yonder.' He inclined his head towards the other side of the street. 'They come in most nights for a drink and a game o' poker.'

'Thanks.'

Rick pushed open the swing doors of the saloon and stepped inside. Everywhere there were lights and noise. He went across to the bar, placed his elbows on it and signalled to the bartender.

He saw the man's eyes widen as he noticed the star.

'You want a drink, Marshal?'

'Whiskey,' Rick said, then lowered his voice. 'Rodriguez and Wesson. Are they in tonight?'

The bartender set a bottle and glass down in front of him. Very quietly, he said:

'They're both in as usual. Sitting at the far table in the corner. You can't mistake the Mex. Wesson is the big guy with the black hair.'

Without turning, Rick surveyed the room behind him in the long mirror at the rear of the bar. He spotted the two men immediately and recognized their kind at once. Hired killers, drifters, willing to use their guns on the orders of the highest bidder.

He turned and leaned back against the bar, sipping the whiskey slowly, knowing that several of the customers were eyeing him closely.

The men at the poker table were talking among themselves in low tones and now he noticed that one of them stood out from the rest. He was dressed in more conservative clothing, steel-rimmed spectacles on his long nose.

Without turning his head, Rick asked:

'The man in the frock-coat. Who's he?'

There was a brief pause, then the bartender murmured softly:

'That's Job Dressier. He's the lawyer in town.'

Rick nodded. 'Guess that figures.' He opened his mouth to say something more but at that moment, the swing doors burst open and a man ran in.

'There's a fire!' he yelled urgently. He seemed to be having difficulty getting the words out. 'Down at the stockyard.'

Within seconds, everyone was stampeding for the doors. Even as he reached them after most of the others had gone, Rick picked out the sound of gunfire in the distance.

The angry orange glow was clearly visible near the far end of the street. Running towards it, Rick guessed there was little anyone could do to save the building. The wooden structure was well alight with flames already licking towards the roof.

'Somebody get some water,' a man yelled. 'We have to try to save the other buildings. If not, it'll spread right through the town.'

As several of the men dispersed along the street there came the sharp bark of rifle shots in the near distance. Almost at once, he pinpointed them as coming from the rear of the blazing building.

He ducked down the narrow alley which ran alongside the stockyard and tugged the Colt from its holster, straining to pick out any movement. Here, the blistering heat of the flames was overpowering.

Smoke caught at the back of his throat, choking him. From not far away, there came a rending crash as a beam fell in and part of the roof collapsed. Eyes streaming, he pulled himself to a halt and pressed himself hard against the further wall. Then a sudden sound at his back brought him whirling round.

A dark figure came running towards him. In the flickering light from the flames, he recognized the deputy, Sanders.

'You see anythin', Marshal?'

'Not a damned thing. But I reckon that whoever started this fire is still out yonder.'

'Who the hell would do such a thing? It ain't Dancroft. He's still locked up in the jailhouse. Unless it's some of his men.'

A moment later, there came the sound of hoofbeats racing along the stretch of open ground a hundred yards away.

Keeping well in towards the wall, Rick ran for the end of the alley.

'There they are,' Sanders muttered. He brought up his gun and fired swiftly at one of the riders.

The next second, Rick joined in. Crouching down, he aimed at a dark shape, saw the other reel in the saddle. For a moment, he hung there, then fell in a sprawling heap on to the ground.

The rest of the riders wheeled their mounts and spurred away into the darkness.

Rick paused only long enough to be sure that the immediate danger was past, then ran forward with Sanders close on his heels. There was no need for him to turn the body over to realize that this was not one of Dancroft's men, nor anyone else from the town.

'An Indian.' Sanders let out a gasp of surprise. 'Goddamn, the Sioux did this. Everyone warned Jordan not to go against 'em but he wouldn't listen, said he'd deal with 'em in his own way.'

Bending, Rick turned the dead man over, then looked up, shaking his head.

'This ain't one o' the Sioux,' he said sharply. 'This is an Apache.'

'An Apache! That ain't possible. There are no Apache in this territory.'

Straightening, Rick said; 'Well, there are now. And I reckon I know where they came from and what they're doin' here.'

'You're sayin' somebody brought them in to burn down the stockyard?'

'That's right. Somebody who wants the Sioux out o' this territory so that he can take over their land.'

'Jordan? But why would he have them burn down his own place? That don't make any sense.'

'It makes damned good sense. He can now get the army in and drive the Sioux out. He'll claim that Dancroft is behind it with some o' the other ranchers. Goddamnit! He can have that building up again within a week. It's a small price to pay for what he really wants, control o' this entire town.'

He noticed the expression of surprise on the other's face which was immediately followed by one of doubt.

'Even if that's true, you'll never be able to prove it.'

'Don't be too sure o' that. Somewhere along the line, he'll make a mistake. When he does, I'll be waitin'.'

Back in the street they found a line of men vainly trying to douse the flames with buckets of water. Corder was there, standing well back as he directed operations. Fortunately, the alley running alongside the stockyard separated the nearest building from those on fire and so far the flames had not spread beyond the gap.

Five minutes later, Jordan came riding up. His face was grim in the ruddy glow of the fire. He walked right up to the sheriff.

'You got any idea who did this, Corder?' he demanded harshly.

Corder shook his head, looking uncomfortable under the other's direct stare.

'We just got warnin' there was a fire, Mr Jordan,' he muttered hoarsely, wiping the sweat from his face. 'By the time we got here there weren't nothin' we could do. The flames had too good a hold.'

'No. Well, by God, somebody is goin' to pay for this night's work.' Jordan swung round to face the crowd that had gathered. 'Any o' you men see anythin'?'

'It were a war party of Indians.' A man pushed his way through the onlookers. 'I just caught a glimpse of 'em over to the back yonder.'

'Indians?'

'That's right.' Rick stepped forward. 'Only before you go off half-cocked, they weren't Sioux. They were Apache.'

Jordan's lips twisted into a derisive line. 'There ain't no Apache around here.'

'No? Well, if you want any proof, there's a dead one lyin' out there at the back. I shot him before he could get away.'

Jordan hesitated. Then he gestured towards one of the watching men.

'Bring that Indian here,' he ordered.

Two minutes later, the man came back dragging the

dead Indian behind him. The man straightened up with a grunt and looked straight at Jordan.

'He's an Apache all right,' he muttered.

Rick noticed the angry expression on Jordan's face but it was gone in a moment. If the rancher was behind this, he had clearly been hoping that all of those attackers had got away.

'Then all this proves is that Dancroft and some of the others are in cahoots with the Apaches,' he snarled.

'Somebody sure is,' Rick said evenly. Glancing at Jordan as he spoke, he knew that the shot had gone home.

'What do you mean by that remark, Marshal?' Jordan demanded.

Rick walked forward a couple of paces until he stood directly in front of the rancher. There was a dangerous glint in his eyes as he said softly, but loud enough for everyone to hear:

'If Dancroft is in with the Sioux and Apache, why would he shoot down three of 'em in cold blood. That's why he's in jail, ain't it?'

'Hell, I don't know what goes on in Dancroft's mind.' Thinning down his lips, Jordan went on: 'I don't know what you got in mind either, Farnham. But this was a peaceable town before you arrived. Mebbe I should inform your superiors of what you're doin' here, overstepping your jurisdiction. Get them to send you back to where you came from.'

'Do that,' Rick answered. 'But I guess you might have to answer some questions and some of 'em you won't like.'

Jordan made to say something further but at that

moment there was a hoarse shout from further along the street.

Turning swiftly on his heel, Rick made out the solitary figure stumbling along the boardwalk. A moment later, he recognized him as the other deputy. The man was holding his hand to his head.

Brushing past Rick, Corder waddled towards the man.

'What happened, Clem?'

'Two men.' The deputy sagged against a wooden upright, held on tightly for a few seconds. 'Hit me over the head before I could stop 'em. They've let the prisoners outa jail.'

'Did you recognize these men?' Jordan asked.

The deputy shook his head, winced as pain jarred through his skull. 'They both had bandannas over their faces. There's two horses gone too. Reckon they'll be well away by now.'

Jordan shouted to one of the bystanders.

'Get the doc to take a look at this man. You, Corder, get a posse mounted up. I want both o' those prisoners brought back – dead or alive.'

'Guess I'll ride with you,' Rick said thinly. 'There's no reason why Dancroft would break outa jail and ride off with that outlaw, Callen, unless he had a gun in his back.'

CHAPTER FOUR

DEATH IN THE SHADOWS

Within ten minutes a posse had been formed. Jordan had placed himself at the front, alongside Corder. They were talking together in low tones as Rick made his way along the street to where his mount was tethered in front of the hotel.

As he approached the narrow alley which ran alongside the building, away from the main street, a low voice called out.

'Lawman, I would speak with you.'

Rick hesitated with his hand on the rail. Peering into the shadows, he could see no one.

The voice came again. 'Lawman. Come quickly.'

Easing the Colt from its holster, he stepped quickly into the alley, alert for trouble. He knew Jordan did not want him to take any part in this manhunt and there could be a gun trained on him from the deep shadows at that very moment.

Moving forward cautiously, he picked out the dark figure standing some three feet away.

'Keep your hands where I can see 'em,' he said in a low, ominous voice.

The man moved forward and with a shock of surprise, Rick recognized the other as the Sioux brave who had led him to Shangawa that afternoon.

'I am Grey Eagle. Three men came out of the jail with Dancroft. They took the trail to Deep Gulch canyon. I believe they mean to kill him there.'

'How do you know this?' Rick asked.

'We hear that Apache have ridden here. Shangawa sent Grey Eagle to follow. I saw the four white men and then came here to find you.'

'Can you take me to this place.'

'I will take you. But we must ride fast without the man Jordan knowing.' The Sioux lifted an arm and pointed back along the alley. 'My horse is there. Bring yours and we will ride that way.'

As he stepped back into the street, Rick saw that the dozen or so mounted men were already moving out. None of them was looking in his direction.

He unhitched the stallion and led it quietly along the alley with Grey Eagle padding silently in the lead. There was a pony waiting on the stretch of open ground at the rear of the hotel.

Grey Eagle swung easily into the saddle and waited while Rick did the same. The Sioux swung his mount and rode swiftly towards the east. The moon had just risen, round and full. It flooded everything with a yellow brightness, giving sufficient light by which to see, but not enough to make out minute details.

They rode through a stand of tall trees and then came out on to the open ground once more. Here, riding a little way in front of him, Grey Eagle leaned sideways and pointed to the ground.

Peering down, Rick was just able to make out the prints of hoofs in the earth.

'This is the path they took,' Grey Eagle said in a low voice. 'The other white men from the town may know where they are going, but if they ride the trail it will take them until the moon is halfway up the sky. We should reach the canyon before they do.'

'I hope you're right,' Rick grunted. He knew that once he hit the trail, Jordan would make the posse push their mounts to the limit. If the posse should arrive at Deep Gulch canyon before he could get Dancroft out alive, the odds were that the rancher's fate was sealed.

The two gunslingers had a big lead on them. He knew nothing of this country and all he could do was rely on Grey Eagle to find the quickest route.

He could still just make out the narrow, twisting track which the Sioux was following but after a while the other cut off across wilder, stonier country. In the distance, hills showed blackly on the skyline, silhouetted against the moon.

Now they rode in silence. Half an hour passed and Rick could feel the tension in him rising swiftly. He doubted if those three gunmen would keep Dancroft alive for long. He would certainly have recognized them and would be a danger to them if he should escape.

Up ahead, perhaps half a mile away, a rocky defile showed directly in front of them, Soon, it was clear that

Grey Eagle was heading straight for this prominent landmark.

A few minutes later the Sioux reined up his mount and lifted his hand for silence. Coming up to him, Rick asked in a whisper:

'What is it?'

The other pointed. 'There is the track leading into Deep Gulch canyon. That is where they have taken Dancroft.'

Rick nodded to indicate that he understood and stepped down. Motioning him to follow, Grey Eagle glided forward like a dark shadow. Cautiously, Rick went after him. There was just the possibility that those gunmen had guessed they might be followed and had set up an ambush.

Silently, they entered the darkness of the defile, edging carefully through it, eyes alert for any movement. If there was to be any ambush, this is where it would be set up for anyone trailing those men.

But nothing happened and at the end they moved out into the open. Here, Grey Eagle threw an arm across Rick's chest, signalling him to remain where he was.

'Stay here, lawman. Grey Eagle will scout ahead.'

Without waiting for any reply, the other moved silently away, disappearing into a jumble of rocks to their left. Rick edged forward a little way, pushing his sight ahead of him as far as he was able.

An instant later, he realized he was standing on the lip of a precipitous drop-off. The ground at his feet fell away almost vertically. A wave of vertigo threatened to unbalance him. Then, with an effort he pulled himself together and stepped back, pressing his shoulders hard against the rock.

There was a sudden movement at his side and a moment later, Grey Eagle reappeared.

'There is a small hollow back there.' He pointed to where the narrow track angled out of sight. 'They are all there. They do not suspect that we are here.'

'Dancroft is still with 'em?'

'He is there. They have tied his hands behind him. Either they mean to shoot him or they will push him over the edge of the canyon.'

Whispering, the Sioux went on: 'Follow me closely. Make no sound.'

They advanced for fifty yards or so. Then Grey Eagle sank down on to his stomach, motioning Rick to do likewise. An inch at a time, they wormed their way forward.

At first, Rick could see nothing which merited all this caution. Then, faintly, he made out the sound of voices coming from straight in front of them. Then he reached the edge of the hollow Grey Eagle had mentioned. Here the ground sloped downward into a natural basin in the rock. The four men were squatted there, clearly visible in the slanting moonlight.

Rick caught sight of Clint Dancroft right away. The rancher was a little apart from the others, his hands behind his back, shoulders against the rocky wall. The other three men had their backs to him, clearly expecting no trouble.

'I say we finish him now and then head back to town before we're missed and anybody connects us with the breakout,' Rodriguez said in a harsh tone. He turned his head towards Callen. 'You, *amigo*, can hightail it out o' this territory.'

'What have you two got against him?' Callen asked.

Wesson uttered a dry laugh.

'We got nothin' against him. This ain't personal. But we're paid to carry out orders. Jordan's orders.'

Callen shrugged. 'Ain't no business o' mine what you do with him.'

Turning his head, Rodriguez said: 'Ain't never heard that you thought twice about killin' a man.'

'You askin' me to kill him?'

In the moonlight, Rick saw Rodriguez grin wolfishly as if the idea appealed to him.

'Sure, why not?' he said contemptuously. 'I reckon you owe Jordan for gettin' you out o' that jail. If we hadn't done that, could be that marshal would have you swingin' from a tree.'

'It don't matter to us how you do it,' Wesson put in. 'Drop him into the canyon or put a slug into him.'

Lying there in the dimness, Rick reckoned he had heard enough. Easing the Colt into his left hand, he signalled to his companion. Without a sound, Grey Eagle melted into the shadows.

Rick waited until he guessed the Sioux was in position, then drew himself to his feet.

'Guess I've heard all I need,' he grated roughly. 'On your feet, all of you and keep your hands well away from your guns.'

He saw the three men start at the sound of his voice. Slowly, they pushed themselves upright.

'You can't take the three of us,' Rodriguez said ominously. 'Whoever you are, I don't think you'd shoot a man in the back.'

'Don't bet on it. Make one funny move and it'll give me the greatest pleasure to cut you three polecats down right here and now. You all right, Dancroft?' Rick flicked his gaze in the rancher's direction.

'I'm all right, Marshal,' replied the rancher.

'This won't do you any good,' Wesson snarled without turning his head. 'The sheriff is on his way here right now with Jordan. You've pushed your nose into his business once too often.'

Without warning, Wesson threw himself down and to one side, rolling over and jerking his Colt from its holster. At the same moment, the remaining gunslingers spun round, just as Rick's Colt spat flame. Callen staggered as the slug hit him in the chest.

For a moment, he remained upright, struggling to keep life in his body. Then he fell forward on to his face and lay still. Twisting, Rick heard lead hum past his head as Wesson fired.

He tightened his finger on the trigger and loosed off a second shot that hit Wesson between the eyes as he struggled to get to his knees.

Too late, however, Rick realized he was standing on the very edge of the slope. The ground beneath his left foot crumbled, throwing him forward, sending him sliding down the slope, the Colt flying from his hand.

He hit the bottom of the hollow hard. Pain jarred along his right arm. For a moment, he could see nothing.

Somehow, he got to his knees. Rodriguez was standing a couple of feet away, the barrel of his gun lined on Rick's chest. In the moonlight, Rick could see the feral gleam in the Mexican's eyes.

'This is where you get it.' Rodriguez grinned. 'I shoot you and this *hombre*, put my gun into his hand, and everyone will believe the two of you shot it out.'

'You won't get away with that,' Rick said thinly. Out of the corner of his eye, he noticed his Colt lying on the rocks a couple of feet away. His chances of getting it and using it were negligible. But he guessed he had to make the attempt, otherwise . . .

Rodriguez stiffened abruptly, stood up on his toes, his eyes wide and staring. A spasm passed through his taut body. The gun fell from his hand and blood gushed from his slackly open mouth. Then, without a sound, he fell forward, hitting the ground in front of Rick. There was an arrow protruding from between his shoulder blades.

Glancing up, Rick saw Grey Eagle standing on the crest of the hollow, his bow in his hand.

A few moments later, the Sioux had scrambled down into the hollow and was helping him to his feet. Then he went over to Dancroft, took out his hunting knife and cut the ropes binding the rancher's hands.

Dancroft rubbed his wrists.

'This is all Jordan's doin',' he said. 'Now he'll get that crooked lawyer, Dressler, to make out I was in on that jailbreak with Callen. There ain't no place around Twin Forks where I'll be safe.'

'There's one place,' Rick said solemnly.

Dancroft glanced up at him in surprise. 'Where's that?'

'With the Sioux. I'm sure Shangawa will hide you there until I can get to the bottom o' what's goin' on.'

He glanced towards Grey Eagle who nodded gravely.

'You will be safe among my people. Even if Jordan or Corder come looking for you, they will never find you.'

Rick made to say something, then stopped as Grey Eagle held up his hand for silence.

A moment later, the Sioux spoke urgently.

'Riders coming quickly in that direction.'

'That'll be Jordan with the posse.' Rick pointed to where the four horses were tethered. 'Take one o' those. Ride with Grey Eagle for the Sioux camp. Better take the north trail. You don't want to run into those men.'

'But what about you?' Dancroft protested.

'Don't worry none on my account. I'll take care o' myself. Now get goin'.'

Rick waited until the two men had ridden off into the darkness and then squatted on the rocks and built himself a smoke. Drawing deeply on it, he sat there until Jordan rode up a few minutes later.

He saw the expression of surprise and barely controlled anger on the man's face as Jordan dismounted.

'How the hell did you get here?' Jordan demanded, fighting to control himself. 'And . . .' He broke off as he noticed the three bodies sprawled on the rocky floor. 'What the hell. . . ?'

'They went for their guns. Guess they weren't as fast as they thought they were.'

'This one has an arrow in his back,' Corder called. He was bending over Rodriguez. He glared at Rick suspiciously. 'Reckon you'weren't alone when you rode here, Marshal.'

'Nope,' Rick replied evenly. 'I had a guide. One o' the Sioux. He'd spotted these men ridin' outa town from the jail. Weren't too difficult for him to trail 'em here.'

'And where's Dancroft?' Jordan asked through tightly-clenched teeth. 'He left town with 'em.'

'Now that's a puzzle. When I got here there were only the three of 'em. My guess is they killed Dancroft once they were clear o' the town. His body is probably lyin' someplace between here and Twin Forks.'

'You're lyin'.' There was a spark of fury in Jordan's eyes. 'There was no reason for them to kill him.'

Rick shrugged. 'There was no reason for them to bust him outa jail along with Callen. Unless there was a chance that, even in jail, Dancroft might find a way o' stirring up the other ranchers against you.'

Jordan swallowed hard. His right hand dropped an inch towards the gunbelt beneath the black frock-coat. Then he withdrew it as he noticed the expression on Rick's face.

'You're goin' to regret this, Marshal,' he muttered harshly. 'You got no right to interfere in our affairs. We got ourselves an elected lawman and your job ended when you shot those two outlaws and brought the other one into town.'

'Where your sheriff put him into jail and then, by some coincidence, Apaches burnt your stockyard and in all the excitement, two o' your boys busted him out.'

'Those two men were not on my payroll.'

'Sure, you'd say that since neither of 'em is ever goin' to confirm or deny it now.'

'Guess you'll never know, then,' Jordan snapped.

Two hours later, even though it was well past midnight, Jordan faced Corder across the table in Corder's office, his features suffused with barely controlled fury.

'I agree this marshal is gettin' too dangerous to have around,' Corder said, rubbing his forehead. 'But . . .'

Sanders spoke from the dark corner of the room.

'Mebbe we should finish him here and now. He's foulin' up everything.'

'That'll do, Sanders,' Jordan snapped in a tone that brooked no argument.

'Then what are we goin' to do with him?' the sheriff queried weakly. 'He's gettin' to know too much for my likin' and how the hell did he find out about Deep Gulch canyon and get there afore we did?'

'Obviously he wasn't lyin' when he said he had one o' the Sioux helpin' him,' Jordan said sarcastically. His eyes narrowed down as a fresh thought occurred to him. It was one he didn't like. 'I want you and Sanders to follow that trail Rodriguez and Wesson took to the canyon. I want every bit of it searched thoroughly.'

'Lookin' for what?' Sanders asked.

'Don't be a bigger fool than you are. Dancroft's body. If they did kill him before they reached the canyon, it's got to be there someplace.'

'And if it isn't?'

'Then he's still alive and I reckon I know where he is.' Jordan took out a cigar and lit it. There was a worried frown on his face as he blew the smoke into the air. 'Trouble is, he's somewhere where we can't easily get at him.'

'Where's that?' Corder asked, puzzled.

'In that Sioux camp. But before worryin' about that, I want to be sure whether he's dead or alive.' He knocked ash from the cigar on to the floor at his feet. 'And right now, it's this federal marshal who's the big problem as far as I'm concerned.'

Scratching the stubble on his chin, Corder sat back.

'I don't think he'll go peaceable. He's got to be stopped permanently.'

'Reckon you got a few men on your payroll who're fast with a gun,' Sanders said. 'Two or three of 'em around the saloon. Shouldn't be too difficult to get him there. Make him draw on one of 'em, and . . .'

Jordan's first instinct was to reject this suggestion but the more he thought about it, the more it appealed to him.

'It's worth a try,' he admitted drily. 'That way, we could make it look legal if anyone should come askin' awkward questions.'

Rick rose at dawn the next morning. He ate an early breakfast, then rode out to the Lazy W ranch. He knew that Anne Dancroft would be eagerly awaiting news of her father. He didn't know whether she was already aware of what had happened in town at the jail but news travelled fast in these parts and he could imagine how she was feeling.

There was no one in sight as he rode into the courtyard. He dismounted, climbed the veranda steps and knocked on the door. It opened a moment later and Anne stood there, her eyes searching his face for any indication of what might have happened.

'My father's dead, isn't he?' she said in a low, jerky voice.

Rick shook his head. 'He wasn't the last time I saw him.'

She stepped to one side and waited until he had

brushed past her, then closed the door.

'Two of the boys came back from town last night. They said Jordan's building had been fired by Indians, possibly Apaches, and that my father had been taken from the jail by some of Jordan's men. Is that true?'

Rick nodded. 'Rodriguez and Wesson knocked out the deputy while everyone else was at the fire. They set that outlaw Callen free and took your father with 'em.'

'Go on,' she urged as he paused momentarily.

'My guess is they aimed to kill him and drop his body into some canyon way out o' town.'

'Then how. . . ?'

'I intended ridin' with the posse but I got waylaid by one o' the Sioux. Seems their chief Shangawa thinks highly o' your father. We trailed 'em to Deep Gulch canyon, gettin' there just before the posse.'

'And. . . ?'

'I shot two o' the critters and Grey Eagle put an arrow into the third. Your father's now hidden somewhere on the Sioux camp.'

Anne sank down into a nearby chair.

'Thank God. I was sure Jordan had had him killed.'

Rick seated himself in the chair opposite her.

'Trouble is – once Jordan satisfies himself your father is still alive, it won't be long before he figures out where he is.'

'The Sioux will never give him up to Jordan – or Corder.'

Rick smiled faintly. 'Mebbe not. But if Jordan brings the army into this, that could be a different matter. All the sheriff has to do is claim the Indians are harbourin' a wanted killer and those soldiers will take the camp apart until they find him.' Rick got up and paced to the window. 'I'd hoped to get either Wesson or Rodriguez alone, when I might have got some answers, but that's out o' the question now.' Pursing his lips, he added thoughtfully: 'But I reckon there might be someone who'd talk.'

'Who's that?' Anne asked.

'That deputy, Sanders. My guess is he's in cahoots with Jordan and Corder. The sheriff's scared but he's in too deep with Jordan now.'

'Then do whatever you have to. I'm not telling you your job but very soon, unless we do something – and quickly – this whole helltown is going to explode in our faces.'

Rick turned and eyed her in mild surprise. There was a hint of iron in her tone which he had never noticed before. Her shoulders were thrown back and there was a directness in her glance which he found oddly disconcerting.

Her cold, rational analysis of the situation forced him to the conclusion that, with her father absent, she intended to fight to keep the ranch. She was a woman with a lot of pride, he thought, and her stay back East had certainly not made her soft. Indeed, he guessed she could be as strong-willed as her father in the face of adverse circumstances.

'If you need any of the hired hands to help you, you only have to ask,' she said calmly.

'It may come to that,' he replied. 'But not at the moment. This is somethin' I have to do alone. I doubt if Jordan is ready yet to make any direct move against you.'

The tight hardness on her face was plainly visible. 'When he does,' she said, tautly, 'he'll find I can handle a gun as well as any of the men here.'

Sweating in the burning heat of the sun, Corder and Sanders rode back into town, tethered their drooping mounts and headed for the nearest saloon. Jordan was seated on the far side of the room with his back to the wall.

As they sat down, he said harshly: 'Well. Did you find anythin'?'

'Nothin',' Corder grunted. He signalled to the bartender to bring a couple of drinks. 'We covered every inch o' that trail. If those men did kill Dancroft, they sure hid the body well.'

Jordan compressed his lips into a hard line.

'One thing's for sure. They'd never have time to bury the body. So I guess that means he's still alive.'

'If he's with the Sioux, they won't give him up easy,' Sanders said.

'Do you think I don't know that?' Jordan rasped angrily. 'But at least, while he's there he can't do anythin' to spoil my plans.'

'Unless he gets word through to his men,' Sanders remarked drily. Jordan uttered a hoarse laugh.

'The Lazy W men are nothin' more than hired cowpunchers and tomorrow I've got men comin' in to start layin' that line from the railroad. I've already arranged for soldiers from Fort Denson to protect 'em if the Sioux do start anythin'.'

Inwardly, in spite of his earlier show of anger, he felt certain that everything would turn out exactly as he'd planned. With three of his fastest guns stationed in the saloon that night, each man knowing what was expected of him, he doubted if the marshal would walk out of there alive.

Once Farnam was out of the way and with Dancroft hiding out among the Sioux like a frightened coyote, he'd have more than sufficient men to take the Lazy W.

None of the other ranchers dared make a stand against him.

Staring across at Corder, he said sharply, 'I want you to get the town committee together. Right now, I reckon it's about time the folk around here know what I intend to do.'

'You might find some of 'em won't like it,' Corder replied. Seeing the look in Jordan's eyes, he went on hurriedly: 'But I'll have them there. Give me half an hour.'

When Jordan walked into the saloon nearly every chair was occupied. Barely half of the men were on the committee, the others were all his own men.

He lowered himself into the chair beside Corder and rapped loudly on the table, silencing the low murmur of conversation.

'All right,' he began, his tone harsh, 'I guess it's about time you all know about how I intend to drag this helltown off its knees. Right now, all of the cattle have to be driven nearly two hundred miles to the nearest market. I aim to change that.'

He took his watch from his waistcoat pocket and made a show of studying it closely. 'In an hour's time, thirty railroad men will be arrivin' in Twin Forks,

They're goin' to run a line around the north of town. Once that's completed we simply load the cattle into trucks and they're shipped back East where—'

'Hold hard right there, Jordan,' called a voice from the other side of the room. 'You say we load the cattle. From what I've heard, it'll only be your beef. The rest of us won't get a look-in.'

Jordan smiled thinly. 'Ain't you forgettin' something, Dexter? So far, I ain't heard any of you willin' to put a stake in it.'

'You know damned well we ain't got your sort o' money,' shouted another man. 'And don't think we're such damn fools we can't see what's behind all these fancy words o' yours. By the time we get our cattle to market they won't be worth half o' what you get. All you want is to drive us off our land and take it all for yourself.'

'That's your misfortune, not mine,' Jordan said decisively.

'And another thing,' Dexter called. 'That land where you're proposin' to build your line. It not only crosses Dancroft's spread but also some o' the Indian territory. You reckon Dancroft and the Sioux are just goin' to stand by and let you ride roughshod over 'em?'

There was a movement at the table next to where Jordan sat. Dressler stood up.

'I think you should know that the law is pretty clear on this,' he said pompously. 'Clint Dancroft is a wanted killer, wanted for the cold-blooded murder of three Sioux. At the moment, since he's escaped from jail, we don't know whether he's dead or alive.

'However, this land of his is forfeit. Where the Sioux

are concerned, my own feeling is that they must not be allowed to stand in the way of progress. If this town is to grow and flourish, then Mr Jordan's way is the only way it'll happen.'

'More fancy words,' Dexter growled. 'And we all know whose side you're on, Dressler.'

'I'm merely statin' the law as I see it,' Dressler retorted stiffly, resuming his seat.

'You want to say anythin' more, Dexter?' Jordan asked with an ominous ring to his tone. He deliberately allowed his gaze to move from the rancher to the bunch of men sitting nonchalantly around three of the tables nearby.

The look was not lost on the rancher.

'You may think you've got everythin' goin' your way at the moment, Jordan. But once you fire up those Sioux, you'll find you've bitten off a lot more than you can chew.'

Jordan gave a derisive laugh.

'Those Indians ain't goin' to make any trouble for me, I can promise you that. Now, if there's nothin' more anybody wants to know, I have important business to attend to at the railroad depot.'

CHAPTER FIVE

MOONLIGHT STAKEOUT

The train carrying the railroad gang arrived at the depot early that afternoon. Jordan was there to meet them as thirty men climbed down on to the platform. The four wagons behind the locomotive were piled high with heavy wooden sleepers and long metal rails.

'Once you get this lot unloaded, boys, come on into town and you'll all get a drink,' Jordan called loudly. 'It'll be on the house.'

One of the men stepped forward. He towered over Jordan. 'The name's O'Leary,' he said roughly. 'There was talk in Dawson Bend that you got a whole heap o' Sioux here who might cause trouble. Is that so?'

'We had a lot o' men killed by those savages while we was buildin' this railroad,' put in a second man. 'Don't want anythin' like that to happen again.'

'Ain't no chance o' that,' Jordan assured him hastily.

'The Sioux are peaceful now. But just in case a few do make trouble I've asked for soldiers from Fort Denson to be on hand. They'll take care of everythin'. You have my word on it.'

O'Leary considered that for a moment, then nodded.

'All right, men, let's get all this stuff off. Then we'll wash the dust out of our throats.'

The work of unloading the wagons took the best part of two hours even with thirty men hauling on the rails. By the time the task was finished, the sun was beginning to dip down towards the west.

Once he was certain that everything had been done to his satisfaction, Jordan led the men into town. He motioned them towards the nearest saloon.

'Drink all you want, boys,' he said as he followed them.

Then he paused as he caught sight of Corder standing on the boardwalk a short distance away, noticed the other signalling urgently.

'I'll join you in a little while,' he called after the men. Then, whirling, he advanced towards the sheriff.

'Somethin' wrong?' he asked.

'Could be trouble,' the other grunted. 'Sanders rode in a little while back. He spotted a horde o' Sioux less than a mile away. They were watchin' the railroad. Reckon they know about those men comin' in.'

Jordan pressed his lips tightly together.

'That note I gave you to take to the fort. You gave it personally to Captain Ford like I said?'

Corder nodded. 'Sure. Just like you told me.'

'Did he say when he could get some soldiers out here?'

'Won't be until late tomorrow. Seems there's a new major just arrived to take over command. His orders are not to make any move that might antagonize the Sioux. It took a lot o' persuadin' for Ford to convince him they might be needed here.'

'Damn. That's all I need, those Indians attackin' before the army gets here.' He made up his mind quickly. 'Get Sanders to ride out and keep an eye on the trail. Any move on their part that he don't like, he's to hightail it back here and let me know. You got that?'

'You want him to stay there all night?'

'All night and tomorrow mornin'. I don't aim to be taken by surprise now that everything's so close to completion.'

Corder nodded and turned away. Then he paused. 'That marshal is back in town. Saw him ten minutes ago.'

'Where is he now?'

'Went into the hotel yonder.'

'Good. Make sure he's in the saloon tonight. Then we'll rid ourselves of one problem.'

'Wouldn't it be easier and quicker to bushwhack him in one o' the alleys?' Corder suggested.

Jordan had already considered that option but after the meeting earlier, he had realized there were too many of the townsfolk against him and what he was doing.

'No. This way it can be made to look like nothin' more than a gunfight. Nobody's goin' to ask any awkward questions about it.'

Standing at the window of the hotel room, Rick watched the activity going on in the street below with a sense of apprehension. Events were now moving far too fast for his liking.

Even though Shangawa had given him his word to keep the Sioux braves under control, the mere fact that Jordan was now pushing ahead with his plan to build that line across their land might make it increasingly difficult to keep the Sioux in check.

If 2,000 of them went on the warpath, not even the army here would be able to stop them. Was Jordan such a fool, so full of his own inflated self-importance, that he really believed nothing would happen?

He'd known men like that before in a dozen small frontier towns, men who figured they could build empires for themselves by viciously suppressing any opposition. Men who now lay six feet under as their fate had inevitably caught up with them. The same would happen to Jordan, but how many good men would go under and die before that happened?

It was now growing dark outside but there was plenty of light spilling from the saloons. He'd seen those railroad men go into them as he had ridden back into town. Once men like that got too much to drink there could be plenty of trouble.

He tightened the gunbelt about his waist, went down the creaking stairs and into the street. Now that the sun had gone down there was a welcome coolness in the air.

A sudden commotion just inside the door of the nearest saloon caught his attention. The next moment, the doors swung open and one of the bartenders came flying out, to land sprawled on his face in the dirt.

Two men emerged after him. Both had Colts in their hands.

'Nobody gets away with callin' me a liar, Colter,' roared one of the men. Aiming his gun, he squeezed the trigger, sending a slug into the dust within an inch of the other's head.

The bartender thrust his hands over his face, and rolled over, trying to get to his feet.

'I didn't mean anythin'.' His voice was high-pitched with terror. 'There ain't no call to kill me. I . . .'

Both gunslicks laughed loudly.

'On your feet,' gritted the second man. 'I reckon he ought to dance for us.' Waiting until the man had staggered upright, his hands still raised, both men lowered their Colts.

Slugs kicked up spurts of dust around the bartender's feet as his legs jerked up and down like a puppet on a string.

Rick stepped across the street. 'All right, boys,' he called loudly. 'You've had your fun. Now put those guns away and go back inside.'

Both men whirled. For a moment, they seemed on the point of making a play for him. Then they noticed the gun in his left hand. Very gently, Rick eased back the hammer with his thumb, holding it there, ready to drop it at a second's notice.

Reluctantly, both men thrust their guns back into their holsters.

'That's better. Now you're seein' sense.' Rick's grin was hard and vicious.

'Weren't nothin' more than a little misunderstandin',' muttered one of the men.

Rick nodded coldly. 'That's the sort o' misunderstandin' that could put you both in Boot Hill. Now get back inside and the next time you want to use your guns, don't try it against an unarmed man.'

Muttering under their breath, the two men turned and pushed their way back through the swing doors.

'You all right, friend?' Rick asked the bartender.

The man put up his hand and rubbed some of the dirt from his face. He grimaced sheepishly.

'I guess so, Marshal. Thanks for buttin' in.'

'What happened in there?'

For a moment, the other seemed reluctant to answer. Then he said shakily; 'They didn't pay for their drinks. When I asked 'em, they said they'd paid and reckoned I'd called 'em liars.'

'They Jordan's men?' Rick asked.

'Yeah, both of 'em. Always ready for trouble.'

'Guess you'd better get back if you still want your job. I'll come in to make sure they don't start anythin' more.'

'Thanks, Marshal.' The man moved inside, swaying a little. Following him, Rick walked to the bar, his keen gaze flicking around the smoke-filled room.

Rick ordered whiskey and leaned on the bar until the drink came. In a low voice, the bartender murmured:

'Those two gunhawks. Watch them, Marshal. They're in here for trouble.'

'I will.' He had already made up his mind about that. There was a nagging little suspicion at the back of his mind but he couldn't force it out into the open and recognize it for what it was.

Surveying the room through the cracked mirror which ran all the way along the rear of the bar, he was able to take in everything going on at his back. Jordan's men were seated at two different tables some distance apart.

The inkling of something being wrong grew stronger. A warning tingle moved along his back. This had all the makings of a trap and he was in the middle of it. Slowly, he ran his gaze over the rest of the room.

Most of the men there seemed to be townsfolk, with a sprinkling of hired hands from the smaller ranches. Over in the far corner he picked out the unmistakable figure of Jeb Dressler. The lawyer was staring moodily straight in front of him, giving the impression that he was totally oblivious of everything going on around him.

'Ain't it about time you rode outa this town, Marshal?'

Rick stiffened slightly but refrained from turning his head. As he had guessed, it was one of Jordan's men who had spoken. There was a sneering smile on his coarse features.

'Guess that's entirely up to me, mister,' Rick said quietly, his tone even, no emotion in it.

He saw the other's grin widen, eyes narrowed into vicious slits.

His companion, several feet away, called loudly:

'We got our own ways here. Sheriff Corder represents the law in Twin Forks. Reckon we don't take to outside marshals ridin' in and tellin' us how we should run our town.'

'Far as I recollect, I ain't seen Corder enforcin' the law around here,' Rick replied. 'Seems to me that all he does is take his orders from Jordan.'

'You ain't got no call to say that,' the nearer man

muttered. 'So far, they say your tally o' dead men is three, all shot in the back without a chance of goin' for their guns.'

'Guess you heard wrong, friend.' Rick was aware that all eyes were now on him, trying to figure out his next move. 'Morgan's brother tried to bushwhack me on the way to the Lazy W ranch. As for Wesson and that Mex, they intended to kill Dancroft and both got a chance to draw.'

The second man laughed loudly, his lips twisted into a sneer.

'That's the talk we expect from a yeller coward who hides behind a marshal's badge.'

Breaking off sharply, the first man went for his gun, side-stepping swiftly. It was almost clear of leather when Rick's Colt spat flame. In the same instant, he swung the Colt and fired again, the slug taking the second man in the chest as he tried to bring his gun to bear on Rick. The first gunslick swayed sideways. One foot caught in his chair as he tried to grab the table to keep himself upright. Then he twisted from the waist and went down. The gun in his fist went off, the bullet gouging wood splinters from the low ceiling.

For a moment, Rick's attention was on the two men. Both now lay sprawled between the tables. But it was this momentary lapse of vigilance which almost proved his undoing.

A shot rang out and Rick felt the white-hot lance of pain as the slug ploughed across his right arm. Swinging round, he saw Dressler standing at the table, a derringer in his hand.

He noticed the look of fear which flashed across the

lawyer's broad features as he realized his shot had not gone home as he had intended. Shaking visibly, Dressler dropped the weapon on to the table in front of him.

Gritting his teeth, Rick walked slowly across the room until he was standing directly in front of the lawyer.

'So you were in on this too,' he said through his teeth. 'Reckon you know I'd be well within my rights to shoot you down for that little stunt you just pulled.'

'Then go right ahead,' Dressler blustered, striving to control his fear. 'Or is it that most folk here would call it murder?'

Rick pulled out the chair in front of him and sat down, keeping his Colt lined up on the other's chest.

'Suppose you tell me what this is all about. That little gunplay in the street with the bartender was all part o' the plan to get me in here.' He smiled thinly. 'Those two gunslingers started that argument to claim I'd been shot in a gunfight. That's right, ain't it?'

'I don't know what you're talkin' about,' Dressler muttered.

'You look unduly worried,' Rick went on. 'No doubt you took your orders from Jordan just like those two. If they failed in their attempt to gun me down, it was up to you to do it.'

'I'm sayin' nothing,' the other mumbled.

'You don't have to.' Rick thrust back the chair and got up. 'It's there on your face for everybody to see.'

He bent down and picked up the derringer. He tossed it across the bar to the bartender.

'Keep this,' he called. 'When he wants it back, he'd better be prepared to use it. The next time he tries anythin' like this, I'll kill him.'

*

Outside the saloon, he examined his right arm. Although it was just a flesh wound and a derringer was not a weapon for a long-range shot, his arm was still bleeding. There was a slowly widening stain on his sleeve.

'Better get the doc to take a look at that, Marshal,' said a voice at his back.

Rick turned to find the bartender standing behind him.

'Where will I get hold of him at this time o' night?'

The man turned and pointed along the street to where a light showed through a small window.

'Reckon he'll still be up.'

'Is he another in cahoots with Jordan?'

The other shook his head vehemently.

'Nope. Doc Forbes ain't got much likin' for Jordan. If he weren't the only sawbones in town, Jordan would have run him outa town long ago.'

'Thanks.' Rick crossed the street and knocked softly on the door of the surgery.

It opened a few moments later and a small, white-haired man peered out at him.

'Somethin' I can do for you, mister?'

'I'm told you're the doctor in this town.'

'That's right. I . . .' The doctor broke off as he noticed the star on Rick's shirt, the blood on his sleeve. 'Come inside. Looks to me as though you've been in a little trouble.'

Rick went inside into the lamplight.

'You'll be the marshal they're all fired-up about,' said the doctor. 'What happened?'

'Two o' Jordan's men tried to go up against me in the saloon. I had to kill 'em both but that snake Dressler had a derringer.'

Forbes motioned him to a chair.

'That figures. They say you've been a thorn in Jordan's side ever since you rode into town. I'm surprised you've lived as long as you have.'

After rolling up Rick's sleeve, he went out of the room, coming back a short while later with a bowl of boiling water.

'Luckily it's nothin' more than a flesh wound,' he remarked. 'I'll clean it for you and put a bandage on. Your arm will be stiff for a couple o' days.'

When the job was done, Rick rose to his feet to leave but the doctor placed a hand on his arm.

'In a way, I'm glad you stopped by, Marshal. There's somethin' I reckon you should know.'

'Go on.'

'I was out at Jordan's place this morning. One of his men broke a leg a couple o' days ago and I went out to see how it was comin' along.'

'So?'

'I heard Jordan talkin' with Ned Robart, his foreman, You probably know there's been some rustlin' of cattle recently. The ranchers reckon their steers have gone over the hill to Jordan's spread but with a sheriff like Corder there ain't no way to prove it.'

'You got proof?'

The doctor shook his head. 'Not exactly. But I did hear enough to know they're plannin' to raid a herd tonight. It's full moon and there'll be enough light for them to see what they're doin'.'

'You know whose herd they mean to rustle?'

'The Lazy W. Dancroft's beef. With him out o' the way, they probably reckon there won't be any trouble.'

Rick thought fast. It still wanted three hours to midnight. If he pushed his mount to the limit, he might just be in time to reach the ranch and warn the men there.

He opened the door and threw a quick, wary glance along the street in both directions.

'You goin' to warn Anne Dancroft?' queried the doctor.

'I have to. If Jordan gets away with this, he'll do the same to all the other spreads. That's what he wants. Not just the cattle, but to force them all out.'

'I suppose it's no good me tellin' you you're in no fit condition to ride all that way tonight.'

'No good at all, Doc.'

Hugging the shadows, he edged along the boardwalk to where his mount stood just outside the hotel. Across the street, he made out the portly shape of the sheriff just inside the saloon. Evidently, Corder had arrived once the shooting was all over. Pretty soon, he'd get word to Jordan that his plan had failed.

Whatever happened, he didn't want anyone seeing him ride out of town. If Corder or Sanders noticed him, they might put two and two together and guess he had somehow got wind of the intended rustling.

Silently, he led the stallion along the alley, waited until he reached the open ground, then made a circuit of the town, hitting the trail at the far end. There was still plenty of noise coming from the saloons and he guessed his departure had gone unnoticed.

Now he let the stallion have its head. Fortunately, it was a sure-footed animal and made no mistakes as he raced along the dimly visible trail. The moon had just risen above the rocky rim of the canyon, throwing long, irregular shadows over the uneven ground.

Half an hour later he arrived at the ranch. There was light showing in a couple of the lower windows as he rode up. Anne answered the door. In the pale light, she looked vulnerable but then he recalled the iron hardness in her manner when he had last seen her.

'What is it?' she asked.

'I've reason to believe Jordan intends to rustle your cattle tonight.'

'You're sure of this?' One look at his face convinced her of his seriousness. 'I can see you are. I'll get the boys together.'

She walked swiftly around the side of the house and threw open the door of the bunkhouse. Glancing over her shoulder, Rick made out at least fifteen men.

'Everybody saddle up,' Anne ordered in a sharp tone. 'Jordan's planning to steal our beef. We've got to get out there and stop him.'

'You got any men watchin' the herd right now?' Rick asked.

'Just two. Sam and Jeth are with them.'

Rick saw one or two of the men hesitate. Clearly, they had no liking for going up against Jordan's hired gunhawks.

'How many of 'em do you reckon there'll be?' asked one meaningfully.

'A dozen, perhaps,' Rick answered. 'Not more. They won't be expectin' any trouble, probably figgerin' there'll only be two or three watchin' the herd through the night.'

'Most of the herd is in the west meadow where those Indians were found,' Anne put in. 'If they come straight from Jordan's ranch, they'll be riding through the pines. If we do drive them off, they'll have to return that way and we'll lose them in the trees.'

'Then I'd suggest we split up,' Rick interrupted. 'Half of us lie in wait for 'em in the meadow, the others cover the trail through the trees. That way, we might be able to finish them all.'

'Good.' Anne nodded. 'Then let's go.'

Rick stared down at her.

'You ain't aimin' to ride with us, are you?'

He noticed the hard, determined set of her jaw.

'Too right, I am. And before you start arguing with me, I'm in charge here now and I can use a Colt or a rifle as well as any of these men.'

'Damnation,' Rick muttered. 'Takin' on these gunslingers ain't no job for a woman, no matter how good you are with a gun. You want to get yourself killed?'

'I'm going,' she declared defiantly. 'And that's an end to it. Now let's move out before all of those cattle are gone.'

Less than half an hour later, they spotted the red glow of the camp-fire in the distance. Two men were seated beside it as they rode up. Surprise showed on their faces in the ruddy glow as Anne dismounted.

'We got word there's going to be a raid on the herd,' she said tautly. 'Jordan's men are on their way right now.'

'Hellfire,' grunted one of the men as he got swiftly to his feet. 'What do we do?'

'We'll be ready for 'em.' Rick motioned the rest of the men forward. 'Five of you move into those trees yonder, off the trail. When they come, let 'em through. You got that?'

'We don't open fire?' asked one.

'Nope. There's too much cover among the trees. They'd pin you down. We want 'em to come through into the valley before they have any idea we're waitin' for 'em.' To Anne, he said: 'You'd better stick with me.' He thought she would object but instead she merely gave an almost imperceptible nod of her head.

Settled down a short distance from the herd, they waited. Midnight came and still the silence held. For some reason, the steers seemed unnaturally restless, as if they sensed that something was about to happen.

Beside him, Anne said softly: 'You're sure they'll come?'

'They'll be here.' Rick tried to force conviction into his tone. It was just possible the doctor had picked up the wrong information, or had misinterpreted what he had overheard.

The sharp bark of a distant coyote echoed from the direction of the hills. It was followed almost immediately by the faint drumming of hoofbeats. Rick turned his head. There was no mistaking the sound and it came from the direction he expected.

'They're comin',' he hissed softly. Pushing his gaze through the moonlight, he watched the ragged edge of the pines half a mile away.

A few moments later, the bunch of riders burst out

into the open, heading straight for the herd. Several began firing their guns into the air, yelling loudly as they lifted themselves in the saddle.

It was clear the rustlers knew exactly what they were doing, circling around the rim of the steers, cutting diagonally through the lush grass to move into the herd at the rear.

From the edge of his vision, Rick noticed the two riders pushing their mounts forward to cut in between the oncoming gunhawks and the herd. Harsh, flat echoes raced across the plain as they opened fire on Jordan's men.

One of the gunhawks reeled in the saddle, slumped sideways, his spurs caught in the stirrups as his mount dragged him across the ground. Now, acting on Rick's orders, the two Lazy W riders swung away.

From somewhere in the distance, Rick picked out a loud warning shout from one of the rustlers. By now they had realized they had ridden into a trap, that they were caught in the open, some distance from the comparative safety of the trees.

'Swing round,' Rick yelled harshly. Three of Dancroft's men turned their mounts, sending them racing around the bulging flank of the herd.

Three of the rustlers immediately broke away from the others and came riding straight towards him. A couple of slugs hummed past his head like angry insects as he ducked low over the stallion's neck. Aiming swiftly, he fired at the riders.

He saw one suddenly jerk upright, his gun falling from his hand. Then the man threw out his arms and pitched from the saddle. The remaining two veered away, only for one of them to drop as a gun went off close to Rick.

Risking a quick glance to the side, he saw that Anne had spurred her mount forward. There was a smoking Colt in her right hand. The third rider was spurring away. This was obviously something these men had not been prepared for.

But if the Lazy W riders thought that all they had to do now was finish off the rustlers, they were wrong. These men were professional killers and had been in tight spots before. They knew all the tricks of their trade.

By now they had recovered from their initial surprise and there were still eight of them in the saddle.

The moon suddenly broke free of a bank of cloud and Rick saw the danger at once. The rustlers were now strung out in a wide arc. Evidently they still hoped to spook the herd and drive them towards the perimeter fence. If they succeeded, nothing would stop the maddened beasts. Signalling to the other Lazy W riders, he urged them forward. Most of them had already seen the danger.

Firing swiftly, they drove down upon the rustlers. For a moment, it seemed their efforts were not enough. Then, abruptly, Jordan's men broke.

The sound of gunfire had now reached a crashing climax. In a loose, ragged bunch, the gunhawks headed for the tree-covered slopes with Rick and the rest of the men close on their heels.

Firing now broke out deep within the trees as the men Rick had sent to watch the trail opened up. Within the dark anonymity of the pines, it was impossible to see exactly what was happening.

Rick slid quickly from the saddle and ran for the trail leading into the trees with six Lazy W men beside him.

Now Dancroft's men had to be careful. In the darkness among the trees it was just as easy to hit one of their own men as the enemy. Crouching down in the thick tangle of thorny bushes, Rick saw the man beside him suddenly lurch and go down.

'You hit?' he asked softly. 'How bad is it?'

The man uttered a low sigh through his teeth.

'I'll make it,' he gasped, biting down on the pain. 'A slug in my leg. Don't worry about me. I can still use a gun.'

'You'd better lie still while we finish these *hombres* off,' Rick gritted.

Cautiously, he lifted his head, peering into the trees on either side. Nothing moved. Then a Colt blasted a little way to his left. Instinctively, he aimed at the position, picked out a harsh gasp as the bullet found its mark.

Keeping his head well down, he called loudly:

'There's no way you men are goin' to get outa here. Throw down your guns and come out with your hands lifted.'

'Go to hell,' shouted a coarse voice. The tone was tight and defiant.

'All right. If that's the way you want it,' Rick called back.

For a few moments, the firing had stopped. Now it erupted again, bullets ricocheting off the trees and thudding into the soft earth.

For ten minutes, the stabbing gunfire continued. At

the end of that time, there was no return fire from the trapped gunhawks. There was a long pause, then one of Dancroft's men called from further along the trail.

'I reckon they're all finished, Marshal.'

'Just stay where you are,' Rick shouted back. 'It could be a trick. Some of 'em might still be alive and waitin' for us to show ourselves.'

The uneasy silence drew out and lengthened into a further five minutes. Then Rick lifted himself and and pushed his way through the impeding undergrowth, his Colt ready, the hammer thumbed back.

He came across two bodies slumped against one of the trees. Turning them over, he knew by the limp way they fell that both were dead.

'I guess they're all finished,' he called. Going further, he found three more of the rustlers.

'One here still breathin'.' The voice came from Rick's left. Skirting the trees, he came upon the Lazy W rider, covering the man with his rifle.

Bending, Rick pulled the gunman to his knees. The man moaned deep in his throat and Rick saw he had been hit in the right shoulder. There was also a bleeding wound on the side of his head.

'What do we do with him?' Rick's companion kept the Winchester trained on the man.

'Guess we take him back to the ranch,' Rick replied firmly. 'Ain't no sense takin' him into town. Once he's patched up, Corder will have him out o' jail in no time. Mebbe we can get him to talk.'

CHAPTER SIX

FATEFUL DECISION

Ed Jordan's face was suffused with anger as he learned of the fate of the men he had sent out to rustle the Lazy W herd. Eyes blazing, a tight scowl convulsed his features as he faced Corder.

'I called you here to tell me that most o' Dancroft's herd was now on my range,' he snapped. 'Instead you tell me they were ready for us and all o' my men are dead. How the hell did that happen?'

Corder cringed visibly. 'I don't know.' he stammered. 'Somehow they must've got warnin'. I swear I never breathed a word of it.'

'Somebody did,' Jordan snarled. 'And somebody's goin' to pay.' He sat down heavily in his plush chair, took out a cigar and lit it with hands that were trembling with fury. 'Goddamnit! Can't anybody do anythin' right?'

Corder stood staring down at the polished top of the deck, unable to meet the other's piercing stare.

'Mebbe one o' your boys talked a little too much in the saloon. Once they get a bit too much to drink, they—'

'And there's another thing.' Jordan gave a violent shake of his head. 'I figgered that nosy marshal would be dead by now.'

'That weren't nothin' to do with me.'

Jordan got to his feet and paced the room a couple of times, hands clasped tightly behind his back. He came to a stop facing the window.

'I want you to check around town. Find out who could've known about last night's raid and who's likely to have talked. Got that?'

'Sure thing, Mr Jordan.'

'And I don't want any mistakes or excuses this time, Fail me again, Corder, and your days as sheriff here are over.' There was no mistaking the threat in the rancher's tone.

Gulping, Corder turned and left. After he had gone, Jordan sat down at the desk to consider his next move. There were two things that had to be done in a hurry if his plans were to go ahead.

First, he'd have the debris removed from where the Apaches had burned down the wooden structure. He was sure there were plenty of men in town who would carry that out for him. Three or four days and that would be completed.

His second task was to get those rails laid. That might be more difficult but the men he had chosen knew their job, all had worked on the transcontinental line which now spanned the entire country. Once the soldiers from Fort Denson arrived, he felt certain they would prevent the Sioux from interfering with the work.

That abortive raid on the Lazy W herd had been a setback. Apart from the fact that he could ill afford to lose all of those men, it meant it might take him a little longer to acquire Dancroft's spread. The tracks would run across a portion of that land and without it in his hands, it would prove difficult to extend the track all the way to the stockyard.

An hour later, he was with the working gang. Already, the ground was being prepared for laying the rails. Satisfied with the progress being made, he stepped from the saddle and made his way to where O'Leary was supervising the work.

'How long do you reckon this is goin' to take?' he asked.

Shrugging, the Irishman said: 'Two weeks, three maybe. Depends on a lot o' things.'

'Such as?'

'If we was to get a big storm before we get the ties in, could wash some o' the sand away. If those Indians yonder should take it into their heads to attack, that wouldn't be good.'

Jordan's gaze followed the other's pointing finger. In the distance, he made out the three braves sitting their ponies on top of a low rise. Even from that distance, he could see that they were Sioux and all were carrying rifles.

'Like I told you, I got soldiers comin' from Fort Denson. They'll keep those critters under control.'

'Sure. But when are these soldiers comin'?'

'They'll be here before nightfall. Just keep these

men on the job. There'll be a big bonus in it for everyone if this track is finished within two weeks.'

Leaving it at that, he went back into town. Twenty minutes later, he had found half a dozen men willing to rebuild the burnt-out wreck of the stockyard. Lengths of charred timber lay strewn over the cattle-pens which had remained undamaged by the fire.

Black dust lay over everything and the acrid stench of smoke still hung in the unmoving air. In spite of this, the actual damage was not as bad as it looked.

Now all he had to worry about was bringing in more men willing to kill when he gave the order. Inwardly, he was still smarting under the setback of the night before. Not a single one of those gunhawks he had sent out to rustle that herd had returned and he could only assume they had all been killed. How many casualties the Lazy W men had suffered he didn't know but he felt sure his own men would have given a good account of themselves.

Indeed, he mused, it was just possible that Anne Dancroft now had only a few men there and, unlike himself, it would not be easy for her to hire more. Maybe it was time he had another talk with her, got her to see sense.

Without hired hands it would be almost impossible for her to run that ranch single-handed. With her father gone, the chances were that she would be amenable to selling the spread and going back East.

With these thoughts in mind, he walked over to the sheriff's office where he found Sanders lounging behind the desk. The other sprang to his feet as he recognized his visitor.

'Somethin' I can do for you, Mr Jordan?' Sanders asked.

'Yeah. You can saddle up and ride out with me to the Lazy W ranch. Guess it's time to have another talk with Anne Dancroft.'

'You reckon you'll be welcome there?' muttered the other dubiously. 'By now, she'll know who those rustlers were workin' for. Could be you'll get a bullet instead of a welcome.'

'I'll take that chance,' Jordan grated. 'Now saddle up.'

'All right. But I still think you're wastin' your time.'

Together, the two men rode out of Twin Forks.

Standing on the veranda of the ranch house, Rick built himself a smoke, lit it, and inhaled deeply. Reviewing the events of the previous night he guessed they had got off lightly. Eleven of Jordan's men killed, one lying in the bunkhouse a hundred yards away. It seemed a small price to pay for two of their own dead and three wounded.

There was a faint sound at his back and Anne came out with a mug of coffee.

'Do you think that Jordan will make another try for the herd?' she asked tightly.

Rick shook his head. 'I doubt it. He could ill afford to lose all those men. Sayin' that, I guess it won't be long before he brings in more. There are plenty of gunslingers willin' to throw in their lot with a big man like him.'

Noticing the worried frown on his face, she said: 'You've got something else on your mind.'

'Just wonderin' what he intends doin' next. As things stand, there are only two things that can stop him building that stretch o' reailroad. The Sioux – and if you refuse to sell him that stretch o' the spread.'

'You can be sure I'll never consider that,' Anne declared heatedly. 'If my father were here, he'd say exactly the same.'

'I'm sure he would.'

'You think he really is still alive?'

Rick nodded. 'You have my word on it,' he said. 'Those Indians respect your father. Shangawa refused to believe those braves had been shot by him. So long as he's with them, he's safe.'

'But how long is that going to be? I'm afraid he'll be worrying so much about me that he might ride back into town, or come here.'

'Your father's no fool, Anne. He knows that if he did that, with Corder as the law here, he'd be strung up without any chance of defendin' himself.'

He finished the coffee and handed her the mug, then turned swiftly at the sound of riders in the distance.

Jordan rode up to the veranda steps and reined his mount sharply. His face assumed an expression of angry surprise as he noticed Rick. For a moment, he was on the point of saying something to him, then choked it back.

He forced a faint smile.

'I heard you had some trouble on the spread, Miss Dancroft,' he said. 'I came to see if there was anythin' I could do.'

'You've got some gall coming here, Jordan,' Anne

said through her teeth. 'It was unfortunate for you we were ready for your hired killers.'

Jordan feigned a look of stunned surprise.

'Believe me, those men weren't actin' on my orders. I knew nothin' about this until I was informed this mornin' by the deputy here.'

'You're lyin',' Rick snapped. 'All o' those men we killed were yours and they rode out from your spread.'

'Now there's no reason to make accusations like that, Marshal,' Sanders interrupted quickly. 'You say these men are dead so there ain't no proof they was actin' on Mr Jordan's orders.'

'That's right,' Jordan went on smoothly. 'You get a bunch o' gunslingers ride into town from God knows where and they're liable to do anythin'. I trust you did kill 'em all. Men like that deserve all they get.'

Before Anne could speak, Rick said:

'Oh, we got 'em all. We made damn sure not a single one got away.'

A look of relief flashed over Jordan's face but it was wiped away almost immediately.

'So why are you here?' Anne asked.

Sitting upright in the saddle, Jordan spread his hands.

'It just occurred to me that with so much trouble goin' on around town and nobody safe from such attacks on their cattle, you might consider the proposal I made to your father. It's a damn good price I'm offerin' for this spread. Plenty for you to go back East and forget all the trouble o' runnin' this place.'

'And my father?'

'Don't know anythin' about him,' Jordan answered.

'I sure don't like sayin' this but my guess is that he was shot by those *hombres* who busted Callen outa jail.'

'We searched every bit o' the trail they took but there was no sign of him,' Sanders said. 'Trouble is, there are plenty of places where they could've put his body where nobody'll find it.'

'I'm afraid you have to face the fact that your pa is dead. That bein' so, how do you figure on runnin' this spread yourself? You know nothin' about ranchin'.' Jordan forced concern into his tone.

Anne bit her lower lip. For a moment, she seemed taken in by the other's argument. Then she shook her head defiantly.

'I'll never believe that until I see his body for myself,' she retorted angrily. 'As for your offer, I've no intention of selling you an inch of this land. If you try to push your railroad across it, I'll blast any man who tries. Now get off this spread and take this crooked deputy with you.'

For an instant, Sanders was about to go for his gun at this insult. His face was flushed and there was an ugly glint in his eyes.

'I wouldn't try it, Sanders,' Rick said, taking a step forward.

'I won't forget this,' the deputy muttered sourly.

He wheeled his mount with a furious tug on the reins. Beside him, Jordan said tersely:

'You've had your chance. Now I'll leave it to the law.'

'Just what do you mean by that?' Rick snapped. A tight smile twitched the other's lips.

'I've had a word with Dressler. Seems the law don't allow a wanted killer to own any land.'

'I wouldn't bank on that. Dancroft was framed for those killings and there ain't been no trial.'

'You got any proof o' that, Marshal?'

'Not yet. But you can be damn sure I'll get some. Then you and these crooked lawmen you've set up in town will be in jail.'

Jordan laughed harshly.

'You're just foolin' yourself, Farnam. By this time tomorrow I'll have enough men in Twin Forks to overrun the town. Take my advice, ride out now. That way, you might save your hide.'

With this threat hanging in the air, Jordan swung his mount and rode out after Sanders.

'He means every word he says,' Anne murmured. 'And he's quite right. I don't think I can manage this spread on my own.'

'You've just got to stick it out for a little longer.' Rick forced reassurance into his tone. 'He may not look it but my guess is that Jordan isn't quite as sure of himself as he tries to appear and we still have one ace in the hole.'

'Oh, what's that?'

'That wounded gunslick we've got in the bunkhouse. Right now, Jordan reckons we killed all of 'em. If we can get him to talk, mebbe we can find out more about what Jordan's plannin'.'

'He'll talk,' Anne said decisively.

'How can you be so sure – and if he does, that he'll tell the truth?'

Anne turned to go back into the house. Over her shoulder, she said, 'Sam Parker, one of the rimriders, spent some time among the Indians. He knows their ways of making people talk.'

*

An hour after noon, thirty soldiers from Fort Denson rode into town, reining up in a long column along the middle of the street. Jordan stepped down from the boardwalk as the officer in the lead climbed out of the saddle.

'Mighty glad to see you and your men, Captain Ford,' he said genially. 'You got my message?'

Ford nodded. 'We passed your working gang on the way in. However, we saw no sign of the Sioux. You're sure they're out to make trouble?'

'Pretty certain. We spotted a number of 'em near the hills. They claim some o' this land is sacred to them. They've sworn to stop us if we set foot on it.'

Ford set his lips into a stiff line.

'You realize that our main duty is to prevent them going on the warpath. That could be catastrophic and Major Reynolds is determined to prevent that at all costs.'

'Naturally. That's also the last thing I want.' Jordan paused. 'There is, however, one other thing you should know.'

'What's that?'

'Three unarmed Sioux were shot down in cold blood by one of the ranchers, a man named Dancroft. The sheriff brought him in and put him in jail until the circuit judge gets here.'

'I see. Then if you'll hand him over to us, I'll have him escorted to the fort. We'll—'

'Unfortunately, that isn't possible.'

'Why not?'

'Two men, almost certainly Dancroft's men, busted him out o' jail and took off with him. My information is that the Sioux are hidin' him in their camp.'

A puzzled frown settled over the officer's bluff features.

'That don't make sense. If he killed three of their braves, why should the Sioux hide him. They're more likely to kill him.'

Jordan shrugged. 'Could be they're not sure if he committed the murders. Dancroft has been on fairly good terms with the Sioux. But whatever the reason, I want you to search that camp and bring him back here to face trial.'

'That isn't going to be easy, Jordan. You know how the major feels about the army interfering in the ways of the Indians. They're now protected by the government and unless they start trouble, there's not much we can do.'

Jordan's face twisted into an ugly expression.

'You owe me a favour, Ford. Now's the time for payback. If that *hombre* is bein' protected by the Sioux, that's against the law. I want him and I want him fast.'

Ford hesitated, then nodded reluctantly.

'All right, I'll take some men there tomorrow. But this will have to be carried out carefully. If those Sioux start anything because of this, my career is on the line. You understand that?'

'Sure. Just do it and make a thorough search of that camp. In the meantime, you can billet your men in the hotel yonder.'

Two nights later, Rick rode out from the Lazy W ranch

and headed north, skirting the town. He had learned a good deal from the wounded gunslick they had captured. Anne had not exaggerated when she had claimed that Sam Parker knew ways of getting information out of people and for once, he reckoned the man had told the truth.

As he had suspected, that arson attack on the stockyard building had been engineered by Jordan. The rancher had somehow formed an uneasy alliance with the Apache and had used them to his advantage. His implication in the raid on the herd was also a fact.

What worried Rick most, however, was the news that Jordan was now convinced that Dancroft was hiding out among the Sioux. Sooner or later, he would insist that the army search that encampment and, if he was found, Jordan would ensure that the rancher never reached Twin Forks alive.

As he rode, he eyed the sky above the tall hills apprehensively.

It would be a wet ride before he reached the Sioux camp, he decided. Towering thunderheads were showing where the last vestiges of the sunset were slowly fading.

The gusting wind which had been blowing all day had now died away completely, leaving the air heavy and oppressive. The approaching black clouds suddenly wiped all of the sunset away and ten minutes later came the warning rumble of thunder in the distance.

As he followed a narrow switchback trail around the lower slopes of the hills, the clinging silence was brought to a head, rather than broken, by the occasional thunderclap.

Soon, the rain came, sweeping from the south-west. Bending low in the saddle, he narrowed his eyes against it, tugging down the brim of his hat to shield his face.

Lightning streaked in whiplash arcs across the heavens. The stallion bucked and reared a little as the thunder racketed and echoed among the hills, forcing him to keep it in tight check.

Once through the hills, the land was more open and there was nothing to afford any protection against the lashing rain. Here there was a vicious savagery about the storm. Although such berserk fury as this was infrequent, when such weather conditions did occur they were bad, and men caught in them often related their experiences afterwards.

In places, the torrential downpour caused the ground to become waterlogged, a surface of slippery mud. Narrow rivulets grew out of nothing and rushed across his path down the hillsides at his back

The Sioux camp still lay some two miles ahead in the all-enveloping blackness. By the time he reached it the rain had soaked through his clothing, dripping continuously from the brim of his hat and running uncomfortably down the back of his neck.

In spite of the tightness in him, he felt a wave of relief as he slipped from the saddle. Ducking his head, he entered the large wigwam.

Shangawa raised a hand in greeting. If he felt any surprise at seeing him there, none showed on his leathery features. Rick seated himself cross-legged on the floor. 'There are important matters we must discuss, Shangawa,' he said. 'You know the army has sent soldiers to guard the building of this railroad around the town.'

Shangawa nodded gravely. 'A captain came here with many men looking for the white man Dancroft. His soldiers searched the whole camp trying to find him. The man Jordan was with them.'

'I hoped that wouldn't happen,' Rick replied soberly. 'Did they find him?'

'No. They found nothing.'

Knowing how thorough those men would have been, Rick found it difficult to understand how they could have failed to find Dancroft, no matter where the Sioux had concealed him.

'Then where did you. . . ?' he began.

There was an expression of sardonic amusement on the old chief's face. 'The soldiers are fools. They look everywhere, seeking a paleface.'

Shangawa clapped his hands sharply. The flap was abruptly twitched aside and Grey Eagle entered. Shangawa said something in the Sioux tongue and Grey Eagle went out. He came back two minutes later with another brave on his heels. Rick stared hard at the second man. Then slowly, in spite of the paint on the other's face, recognition came.

'Dancroft!'

The rancher nodded. 'Those men were completely fooled' he said evenly.

'Evidently,' Rick said. 'But now we must talk. Jordan is gettin' that crooked lawyer, Dressler, to draw up papers claiming that a wanted killer has no title to any land. He tried to force your daughter's hand but she's got as much grit as her father.'

Dancroft's face hardened.

'He's the biggest killer in the entire territory,' he rasped. 'While there's a breath in my body, there's no way he's takin' my land.'

'Dancroft is blood-brother to the Sioux,' Shangawa said softly. 'Already, this man Jordan is seeking to take our land. Soon, he will force us into the hills, kill all of the buffalo. Shangawa believes it is time for the Sioux to fight.'

'No! That would play right into his hands. If you went on the warpath against those railroad men, or the soldiers, the army would send many more soldiers. They'd crush you and that's what Jordan is hopin' for.'

'Then what do you suggest?' Dancroft asked.

Rick paused for a moment, then said:

'I want you to come back with me to the ranch. I know it's mighty dangerous but somehow we've got to get all of the other ranchers to band together and stand up to Jordan.'

Dancroft evinced no hesitation.

'All right, I'll do it. But it won't be easy convincin' the others.'

Turning to Shangawa, Rick asked: 'How well can you control your warriors?'

'They will all obey whatever Shangawa says' replied the chief.

'Good. If we can delay the layin' of these tracks, we might be able to force Jordan's hand. At sunrise tomorrow, get all of your braves and ride out to that stretch o' railroad. I figure those men there will think twice if they figure you're goin' to attack.'

'You're goin' to force a stand-off?'

Rick nodded. 'It might give us a little time.' He forced a faint grin. 'Believe me, right now we have very little left.'

CHAPTER SEVEN

ROUGH JUSTICE

Rick reined his mount on a low rise half a mile from town. From this vantage point he was able to see just about everything in Twin Forks. It was almost two o'clock in the morning and down below scarcely any lights were visible.

Overhead, the storm had moved away and much of the sky was clear and starlit. A chill wind was still gusting, however, blowing from the distant heights.

Slowly, he ran his keen gaze over the main street, a long ribbon of grey, and the buildings clustered on either side. As far as he could see, nothing moved. There were no shadows visible that had no right to be there.

At last he was satisfied. Turning to his companion, now garbed in his own attire, he said softly:

'I don't think this is wise, Clint. Why do you have to put your neck into a noose if we're seen?'

Dancroft's lips twisted into a grim smile but there was no mirth in it.

'Because after all that's happened, I intend to have it

out with that crooked lawyer and this is as good a time as any. If he's aimin' to draw up so-called legal papers to force me off my land, then I aim to stop him.'

'Just so long as that's all you do and keep your hand away from that gun. I know how you feel and I don't blame you. But if you was to kill him, I'd have to arrest you for murder. You understand that?'

The grimness in Rick's tone was not lost on the rancher.

'Don't worry, I'm not figgerin' on doin' anything like that.'

'Good. Then let's go see if we can rouse him without bein' seen.'

Dancroft gigged his mount forward.

'Ain't likely to be anyone around at this time o' the mornin',' he muttered.

On reaching the end of the trail they walked their mounts along the dusty street, making as little noise as possible. As he rode, Rick kept his gaze on the dark alleys which opened out on either side. There was no light on in the lawyer's office but that didn't guarantee that the lawyer was asleep.

Rick dismounted outside the two-storey building and climbed on to the boardwalk, motioning his companion to keep well in to the wall. If Dressler should spot Dancroft it was highly unlikely he would open the door.

He knocked softly on the door and waited for a couple of minutes. He was on the point of knocking again when one of the upper windows opened. Glancing up, he saw the lawyer's face framed in the opening.

'Who the hell is it?' Dressler called. 'What do you want?'

'Marshal Farnam,' Rick answered, keeping his voice low. 'I have to talk to you.'

A pause, then: 'Do you know what time it is? Can't it wait until a decent hour?'

'It's about Dancroft. I figger it's somethin' you should know.'

This time there was a longer pause and Rick knew he had aroused the other's curiosity.

'I'll be down in a couple of minutes – and this had better be important.'

The window was closed and a little while later Hick heard the faint shuffle of feet inside. There was the unmistakable sound of a bolt being withdrawn and then the door opened a couple of inches.

'Well, what is it? What's so important that—'

The lawyer broke off sharply as Dancroft stepped into view. Seeing him, Dressler attempted to close the door but before he could do so, Dancroft thrust it open. As the lawyer fell back against the wall, the two men brushed past him. Rick closed the door behind him.

In the light of the lamp that Dressler carried, Rick saw the expression of apprehension which flashed over the lawyer's features. In the light, his face looked ghastly.

'Inside,' Dancroft said, nodding towards the door which led into the office. 'And no noise if you want to stay alive.'

'Whatever you've got in mind, you won't get away with it,' Dressler blustered.

'Put that lamp on the desk and sit down,' Rick ordered. 'We're goin' to have a little talk concernin' certain papers you've drawn up for Jordan.'

Dressler slumped into the chair. 'I don't know what the hell you're talkin' about,' he muttered.

'No?' Towering over the other, Dancroft leaned forward across the desk. 'We've heard otherwise. Now start talkin' and it had better be the truth.'

Swallowing hard, his Adam's apple bobbing up and down nervously, Dressler's gaze darted from one man to the other. His eyes widened as he saw the rancher's hand move down towards his gunbelt.

'All right, all right,' he said jerkily. 'Jordan asked me to draw up a document claimin' that since you're a wanted killer, you got no legal entitlement to the Lazy W spread.'

Dancroft glanced sideways at Rick.

'You heard of any law like that, Marshal?'

Rick shook his head. 'Nope. And since you were framed for those killings, in my opinion you're innocent until proved guilty.'

With an effort, Dressler forced himself upright. There was now a cunning look at the back of his eyes.

'I don't know where you've been these last few days, Dancroft, and I guess it ain't any business of mine. Jordan and the sheriff spread it around that you were dead.'

'And dead men don't cause any trouble.' Straightening up, Dancroft said harshly: 'Unfortunately for Jordan, I'm still alive and there ain't no way he's gettin' his hands on my ranch. Now I want that document you've made out.'

Dressler spread his hands.

'It ain't here. I gave it to Jordan. If you want it so

desperately, I guess you'll have to talk to him about it.'

'You're lyin' through your teeth, Dressler,' Rick grated thinly. 'Now get those papers pronto. We don't aim to stick around here all night.'

Dressler hesitated, then shrugged resignedly. He reached down, pulled open a drawer in his desk and put in a hand. With a jerk, he drew it back, and the lamplight gleamed on the derringer.

But Rick had been expecting something like this. Before the lawyer could lift the gun, his left fist slammed down hard on Dressler's wrist. With a yelp of pain, the lawyer released his hold on the weapon.

'I figgered you might try somethin' like that,' said Rick. He picked up the gun, unloaded it and slipped the slugs into his shirt pocket. He placed the derringer back on the desk.

Seeing the look in the lawman's eyes, Dressler fumbled inside the drawer, then brought out a couple of sheets of paper. Dancroft snatched them up and studied them closely. Then he nodded, satisfied.

'You're goin' to regret this night's work, both of you,' Dressler snarled viciously. He was getting some of his old bluster back now that he felt reasonably certain these men did not intend to kill him. 'In your hands, Dancroft, that document ain't worth the paper it's written on. I can easily make out another.'

Dancroft pursed his lips.

'Mebbe there are other papers in that drawer you wouldn't like to fall into the wrong hands,' he said.

He moved around the side of the desk and drew out several sheets. He bent to examine them. He uttered a low whistle. 'Seems this snake of a lawyer has been mighty busy over the years,' he said. 'These are all deeds made out to Jordan and all pertain to spreads that were taken over by him.'

'We'll take 'em with us,' Rick told him. 'They'll come in handy when the circuit judge gets here.'

'They won't make any difference when he does,' Dressler muttered, a note of growing confidence in his tone. 'You're finished, Farnam. Concealin' and protectin' a killer. I wouldn't give a plugged nickel for your chances in front o' Judge Benson.'

Rick placed his hands flat on the desk and stared down at the lawyer.

'That's where you're wrong. You see, I sent a message to Denver this mornin'. Seems they now know quite a lot about Benson, that he's been in cahoots with Jordan for years.

'This time, it'll be Judge Wesley. Unfortunately for Jordan's plans, he happens to be a straight, honest man who can't be bought. Jordan won't be able to bribe him.'

From the expression on the lawyer's flabby features, he knew this shot had gone home.

'Now I suggest you just sit there until we've gone. Try to give a warnin' and it' be the last thing you do.'

Rick and Dancroft let themselves out into the streets, climbed into their saddles and headed along the trail leading to the ranch.

Behind them, the street seemed as empty and deserted as when they had ridden in only a short while earlier. But no sooner had the two riders vanished into the distance than a dark figure detached itself from an alley-mouth only a few yards away.

Jordan had seen the two men ride into town. He had spent several hours in deep conversation with Ford going over the details for protecting his gang from any possible Indian attack.

When he had seen them enter the lawyer's office it had immediately excited his curiosity. Recognizing Dancroft had brought a sense of surprise. Where those Sioux had concealed him was something he couldn't fathom.

Yet he now no longer doubted that Farnam and the Sioux chief had been in on the plan to keep Dancroft out of sight.

He strode along the boardwalk until he reached Dressler's door. It was open and he walked in, finding the lawyer slumped in the chair behind the desk. His gaze fell on the derringer lying in front of the lawyer.

Dressler glanced up sharply as Jordan advanced towards the desk, pulled out the chair and seated himself.

'I see you've had visitors, Jeb,' he said gruffly. 'Mind tellin' me who they were?'

'If you know that much, you know damn well who they were,' Dressler snapped. 'That nosy marshal and Dancroft.'

'And what exactly did they want?' Jordan asked smoothly. 'I'd figgered that Dancroft was dead. Seems I was wrong.'

'Word must've got to him about those papers I'd drawn up, orderin' that land to be put up for public auction.'

'And did he get 'em?' Jordan's tone remained calm and even but there was a bite of iron in it which

Dressler noticed at once.

'I tried to stop him but he was too quick for me.'

Jordan lit a cigar and cleared his throat.

'No harm done. They won't do him any good, but—'

'This plan of yours won't work; we've gone too far this time.' The lawyer's words came out in a rush. 'Farnam's got most o' the other deeds goin' back for several years.'

Speaking around the cigar, Jordan said: 'You worry too much, Jeb. I don't aim to let anythin' stop me now.'

'No? Then I reckon there's somethin' you should know. The circuit judge is due here in three days and it ain't Benson. Somehow, Farnam got a message off to Denver this mornin'. Judge Wesley is on his way here and there ain't no way you can bribe or intimidate him.'

'Wesley?' For the first time, Jordan looked stunned by what he was being told. 'You sure o' that?'

' 'Course I'm sure. That's why I'm gettin' out o' this. When the next stage arrives in town, I aim to be on it. I don't intend to stick around and put my head into a noose.'

'I hope you're not thinkin' of runnin' out on me, Jeb. That would be extremely foolish.'

'If you've got any sense, you'll take your money and ride. From what I've heard, that judge has strung up bigger men than you.'

'Nobody takes what's mine. I've fought too long and hard for this. And if you're thinkin' of quitting, you'd better think again. We're both in this, together, to the end.'

With a sudden swift movement that took Jordan by surprise, Dressler snatched up the derringer, acutely aware that the hand which held it was shaking.

'Don't make me use this, Jordan. Unlike you, I don't want more blood on my hands but I'll shoot if I have to.'

Smoothly, in spite of his bulk, Jordan got to his feet. There was a sneering smile on his face.

'You won't pull that trigger. You don't have the guts to shoot a man in cold blood.'

Slowly, Jordan reached inside his frock-coat for the Colt concealed there. He drew it out.

Too late, Dressler recalled that the marshal had emptied the gun before he left. Jordan jerked instinctively as the hammer fell on the empty chamber in the derringer.

Then, his teeth bared in an animal-like grimace, he squeezed the trigger of his Colt. Dressler staggered back under the impact of the heavy slug in his chest. His back arched over the chair. Then he toppled back, taking the chair with him. He fell to the floor with his legs twisted unnaturally under him and stared sightlessly at the ceiling.

Acting quickly now, knowing that the shot would soon bring someone running to investigate, Jordan ripped open the drawers of the desk, scattering the papers all over the floor.

Within seconds, he was outside. A swift glance in both directions told him that the street was still empty. He slipped into the nearby alley and moved quickly and silently along it.

On reaching the end he paused, hearing a sudden shout from the direction of the street. Three minutes later, after circling around the backs of the buildings, he emerged, unseen, from the darkness at the side of the lawyer's office.

*

On this occasion, Sheriff Corder led the posse along the trail to the Lazy W ranch. He didn't anticipate any trouble bringing in both Dancroft and the marshal. This time, Farnam wouldn't be able to hide behind his badge.

The evidence against Dancroft for the killing of those Sioux braves was certainly circumstantial. But as far as Dressler's slaying was concerned, the case was rock solid. After questioning most of the townsfolk, he had found himself a reliable witness.

One of the soldiers billeted in the hotel had been woken during the night by the sound of horses moving stealthily along the street, just outside the hotel. Curious, he had gone to the window and, in the darkness, had picked out the two men riding cautiously into town as if they had no wish to be seen.

His description of one of them tallied closely with that of Clint Dancroft and he had been fairly sure that the other wore a star on his shirt.

Thinking that the lawman was bringing in a prisoner, he had returned to his bed. He had been on the point of falling asleep again when the sound of a single shot had brought him bolt upright. Of one thing he was certain, however. The two riders had dismounted outside the two-storey building on the opposite side of the street.

When they were within a mile of the ranch, Corder called out to the men riding behind him.

'Keep your eyes open. If I know Dancroft, he'll have men posted along the trail.'

'I reckon we can handle them if they dare show their faces,' Sanders said viciously.

'Don't get too confident,' Corder muttered. 'He might make a fight of it before we take him in.'

'Dead or alive?' queried one of the other men.

'Either way. Makes no difference to me.' Corder wiped the sweat from his face where it was dripping into his eyes. He normally left the riding to his deputies, but on this occasion he wanted to be in on the finish.

They sighted the ranch house ten minutes later. There were no mounts visible and that made Corder suspicious. Either the Lazy W riders were all out watching the herd, or he and his men could be riding into a trap.

With a jerk on the reins, he pulled up his mount directly in front of the door. Easing himself more comfortably in the saddle, he called:

'I know you're in there, Dancroft. You too, Marshal. Now step out here with your hands lifted.'

When there was no reply, he opened his mouth to yell again but at that moment Anne Dancroft came out to stand on the veranda. She folded her arms.

'What's your business here, Corder?' she said, coolly.

'You know damn well why I'm here. To take your pa and the marshal in for the murder o' Jeb Dressler.'

He noticed the expression of stunned surprise on the woman's face and guessed that she knew nothing about the killing.

'If Dressler's dead, why should my father have anything to do with it?' she demanded heatedly.

'It's all right, Anne. Let me do the talkin'.' Dancroft stepped outside.

'There ain't nothin' you can say, Dancroft.' Corder

leaned forward in the saddle, his right hand close to the Colt at his waist. 'You shot Dressler last night and Farnam was with you when you killed him.'

Edging his mount forward a little way, Sanders said harshly:

'We got a witness who saw both of you ride into town early this mornin'.'

'Another o' your paid informers, I suppose,' Dancroft retorted.

'Nope.' This time Corder spoke, a note of sardonic satisfaction in his voice. 'One o' the soldiers billeted in the hotel. Reckon you'll find it hard to deny his evidence.'

'I ain't denyin' anything. Sure, I paid a visit to the lawyer this mornin' with the marshal. I forced him to hand over those so-called legal documents strippin' me of this land. But he was alive when we left him.'

Corder uttered a coarse laugh.

'Sure he was. Only I don't reckon there's any jury who'd believe that. They're more likely to believe you got your hands on those documents and then you figured Dressler could easy write some more, so you had to stop him permanently.'

He turned his head slightly and signalled to Sanders and the others. 'Hogtie him and put him over one o' the horses. Then search this place for Farnam. I want 'em both. If they make a wrong move, shoot 'em.'

Before any of the men could make a move, Rick appeared in the doorway. Both he and Dancroft now had guns in their hands.

'You'll be the first to die, Corder,' Dancroft said harshly.

Corder bit his lower lip, then forced a grin.

'You can't shoot all of us. We'd get all three of you before you did that. Better think o' your daughter, Dancroft. She's right in the line o' fire.'

'You'd all be dead before your guns cleared leather,' Anne said evenly. 'Right now, there are a dozen rifles trained on you. One move the boys don't like and you'll get a bullet where you won't like it.'

'You're bluffin'.' This time there was doubt in the sheriff's voice. Then, turning his head slightly, he threw a quick look around the courtyard. The sunlight struck bluely off the barrels of Winchesters in the windows of the house, barns and livery stables.

'Damn you, Dancroft,' he snarled. 'You'll all pay for resistin' the law. This is the finish for the lot o' you.'

For an instant the fury that flared inside him was so strong that he was tempted to order the men with him to gun down the three on the veranda. Then sanity prevailed. Choking down his chagrin, he jerked viciously on the reins, turning his mount.

'I'll be back,' he rasped thinly. 'And the next time, there'll be sufficient men with me to overrun this place and everybody in it.'

As he put his mount to the downgrade, Anne called sharply:

'When you do come, be ready to use your guns.'

Out of the corner of his eye, Rick studied the girl's features as she stared after the riders. It seemed impossible she could have changed so much since that day he had first seen her on the train.

There was a hardness in her, a grim determination, which he had never expected.

She turned and flashed a brief smile at him.

'They'll come back,' she said. 'Being beaten like this won't settle well with Jordan and he won't be too pleased that he's failed again.'

As they went inside, Dancroft said uncertainly:

'Who do you reckon shot Dressler? Whoever it was must've killed him only minutes after we left.'

'I guess we don't have far to look for the killer,' Rick said quietly. 'Either Jordan or one of his men.'

'But why Dressler?' Anne asked. 'I thought those two were in this together.'

Rick gave a nod. 'Sure they were.' To Dancroft, he went on: 'But did you see the look on Dressler's face when I told him Judge Wesley was on his way here. I'd say he's been thinkin' of pullin' out for some time and that was the last straw.

'If he told Jordan he wanted out, he sealed his own fate. Jordan would never let any man run out on him. Besides, Dressler knew too much and he could be dangerous if he talked. That's why he had to be silenced.

'Just too bad Corder found that witness. Now neither of us can show our faces in Twin Forks. I guess this is the only safe place for the time bein'.'

'Does that mean we're holed up here, doing nothing?' Anne said. 'Waiting for Jordan to make his play.' There was a note of desperation in her voice.

Shaking his head, her father hitched his gunbelt higher about his waist.

'There's only one course open to us. I've got to get the other ranchers to back us and if we're to have any chance o' succeedin', we have to act fast. If we can hit

Jordan while he's still preoccupied with that railroad around town we might have a chance.'

'What do you intend to do, Rick?' For the first time, he noticed a look in her eyes which hadn't been there before.

Rick's face was set in tight, grim lines.

'Now I'm certain Jordan knows about Judge Wesley, I've got to make sure he gets here alive because Jordan will do everythin' he can to stop him.'

'You mean he might try to bushwhack the stage and have him killed?'

'Where Jordan's concerned, anything is possible.'

Out on the edge of town, the line of gleaming rails was gradually extending north. Soon, O'Leary reckoned, it would be encroaching on Indian territory and he was still unsure of Jordan's ability to protect him and his men if the Sioux did make trouble.

He had seen the group of cavalry ride in the previous day but to his way of thinking, thirty or so soldiers were no match for a couple of thousand Indians if they went on the warpath.

Now, as he walked slowly along the track, surveying the men knocking in the ties, carefully making sure the gauge was correct, he could feel the tension beginning to rise. Cursing and sweating, the men hammered the rails into position.

All except himself were stripped to the waist, their bodies burned a deep copper from long exposure to the sun. Only the thought of the bonus which Jordan had promised kept them at it with scarcely a halt.

The storm of the previous night had not caused as

much delay as he had feared. They had caught the edge of it and the lashing rain had washed only a little of the sand and earth out of place. Now, in the blistering heat of the noon sun, everything seemed to be going to schedule.

One of the men straightened up with a grunt, pulled out a rag and wiped the sweat out of his eyes.

'You're sure this man Jordan knows what he's doin'?' the man asked. 'He says those Sioux won't attack once we cross on to their land but I've had dealings with these tribes before when we were layin' the railroad across Colorado. We must've lost near on a hundred men before the army drove 'em off.'

'They've kept away so far,' O'Leary answered. 'If Jordan's so sure about it that he's still stickin' around, guess he knows what he's talkin' about.'

'And what about those who burned down his cattle yard?'

'They were Apache, a renegade band. There weren't more'n a score of 'em. These others are the Sioux and they've been at peace for years.'

'And you still think that they'll—' The man broke off sharply. There was an expression of shocked surprise on his leathery features. He was staring at something over O'Leary's shoulder.

The other turned slowly, not expecting what he saw. Fanned out on the far side of the main railroad track, row upon row of Sioux sat their ponies in absolute silence. There had been no indication of their arrival. None of the men had heard a sound.

'What the hell. . . ?' Somehow, O'Leary got the words out. He uttered a throaty shout to the rest of the men.

'Stop what you're doin'. We got company.'

'Christ Almighty:' muttered one of the men. 'You think these critters mean business?'

'They mean trouble, all right,' O'Leary said. 'Where the hell are Jordan and those troops?'

It was ten minutes later before Jordan and Captain Ford rode up. The latter ordered his troopers to spread out in a long line.

Ford cast an apprehensive glance in the direction of the Sioux. It was clear from the look on his face, and the way he held himself rigidly in the saddle, gloved hands clenched tightly around the reins, that he did not relish the thought of going up against them.

'You goin' to do anythin' about those Indians?' O'Leary asked sharply.

Ford licked his dry lips.

'First, I aim to find out what they've got in mind,' he said stiffly. 'Guess I'd better go and talk with them.'

Jordan hesitated, then said: 'I'll ride with you, Captain.'

The other's face indicated that he was not pleased with this suggestion. Nevertheless, he gave a curt nod of acquiescence.

'Very well. But I'll do all the talkin'.'

Prodding spurs into his horse's flanks, he urged it forward, across the tracks, to where Shangawa sat impassively on his mount. He raised his right hand in greeting.

'We come in peace, Shangawa. Why do you bring all of your warriors here?' Ford said slowly.

Shangawa lowered his lance until it was pointing directly at Jordan.

'This man who speaks with forked tongue against the Sioux comes to steal our sacred land so that the iron horse will ride over the place of our forefathers,' he replied.

'You cannot stop progress because of some old myths and superstitions,' Jordan butted in. 'That land belongs to the American people, and anyone strong enough to hold it, not to—'

'Hold your tongue, Jordan.' Ford's words crackled like sparks. 'The army will deal with this.'

'Then go ahead and deal with it,' Jordan muttered ominously. 'But just remember why you're here. To make sure that track is laid and those men back yonder are protected.'

There was a sharp retort on the captain's lips but he bit it back with an effort.

He turned his attention back to Shangawa.

'This is a time for wisdom, Shangawa,' he said smoothly. 'If you were to attack any of those men, word would be immediately sent to the fort and also to the army post in Denver. More soldiers than you can imagine would be sent and your entire people destroyed.

'The railroad will not harm the Sioux. There is plenty of land to the north. The buffalo will still roam the plain. Take your warriors back to your camp and consider my words well before you bring death to your people.'

Shangawa's face remained impassive. Not a single flicker of emotion was visible. Eventually he spoke.

'I will consider your words but my warriors remain here. I do not trust this man who rides with you. His words are false.'

'Why you damned—' Jordan's face suffused with anger at this insult, and his hand snaked downward for his gun. It had almost cleared leather when Ford's steel-like grip stopped him.

'Do you want to get yourself killed, you damned fool?' the captain hissed. 'Pull that gun and you'll have an arrow in you before you can use it.'

Reluctantly, Jordan allowed the Colt to fall back into its holster.

As they rode back across the track, Ford said quietly:

'It may be that Shangawa will see sense. In the meantime, however, you'd better call off your men. If you continue laying that track before I get word to the major I won't be responsible for the consequences.'

CHAPTER EIGHT

KILLER TRAIL

Seething with rage, Ed Jordan stormed into the sheriff's office, slamming the street door shut behind him. Corder and Sanders were both there, had been conversing together in low tones, a conversation which stopped abruptly as Jordan came in.

'Somethin' wrong?' Corder asked, a trifle nervously.

'Every damned thing has gone wrong,' Jordan seated himself at the desk. 'You got a drink here?'

Keeping an eye on him, Corder reached for the bottom drawer and brought out a bottle of whiskey together with a glass. He slid them across the top of the desk.

Jordan spilled whiskey into the glass and gulped it down in a couple of swallows. He filled the glass again and stared moodily at it.

'That damned yeller fool of an army captain,' he grated. 'I brought him here to make sure there was no problem with the Sioux. Instead, he caved in to 'em, made me stop the track-laying. Now it could be weeks before he gets more men and the job can start again.'

He sat in angry silence, swirling the liquor in the glass, his face a mask of ill-concealed fury.

Lounging against the wall, Sanders said:

'There's word that Farnam has sent for a new judge. They say he can't be—'

'I know all about Judge Wesley,' Jordan snapped. He sipped more of the whiskey. 'I've already taken care o' that. Wesley won't get any further than Twin Peaks. Five o' the boys are ridin' out along the Denver trail. That stage might reach Twin Forks but Wesley won't be on it.'

A wolfish grin spread over the deputy's face. 'I get it. There's goin' to be a hold-up somewhere along the trail and Wesley's goin' to get a bullet.'

Jordan finished the rest of the drink, then paused as a fresh thought struck him.

'Where are Dancroft and that marshal? You got 'em locked up in one o' the cells?'

Corder stared down at his hands, then picked up the bottle and took a couple of deep swallows,.

'Well?'

'We ran into a whole heap o' trouble at the Lazy W.'

'What sort o' trouble? You tellin' me you didn't bring 'em both in?'

'Somehow, they got word we were comin'. There were a dozen rifles on us when we tried to take Dancroft and Farnam.'

'So you rode out with your tails between your legs like coyotes.'

Jordan slammed his clenched fist on to the desk. A deep color etched his taut features, the veins standing out across his forehead. 'I warned you, Corder, what would happen if you failed me again.'

Before the other could move, Jordan reached across the desk and ripped the star from the lawman's shirt. 'I got no use for a sheriff who can't carry out my orders. You're finished. Get out o' my sight.'

Corder jerked back in the chair, then floundered to his feet. For a moment, he seemed about to say something in his defence, then he edged around the desk and stumbled out, closing the door behind him.

Deliberating, Jordan stared down at the badge in his fist, then tossed it across the room to Sanders.

'From now on, you're the sheriff here. Guess you're the only one I can trust.'

Grinning waspishly, the other took off his own badge and pinned the other in its place. 'You can rely on me, Mr Jordan,' he said thinly.

'I hope so. I don't know what Dancroft has in mind but he won't be standin' still, doing nothin'. I want you to be ready once I get word that Judge Wesley is no longer a threat. Then you get together all the men you can and crush Dancroft.'

'Won't take me long to do that,' Sanders replied confidently. 'I could be ready to hit 'em tonight.'

Jordan shook his head. 'I've got to be sure that Wesley is dead before I make that move. Wesley seems to know somethin' of what's goin' on here and we could be answerin' a heap of awkward questions. I'll give the word when it's to happen.'

'Sure thing. You're the boss.'

'That's right and don't you ever forget it.'

Still smarting over Jordan's actions, Corder made his way along the street to the nearest saloon. He needed a drink and a chance to think clearly, to decide what he should do next. Not only had he lost his job but his pride had been hit and that rankled.

Pushing open the swing doors, he stepped inside. As he knew from past experience, this was the slack time with only half a dozen men in the saloon.

Four were seated around the table in the corner playing faro while two stood propping up the bar, drinking and saying nothing.

He gave them only a cursory glance, then stepped up to the counter.

'Whiskey, Sheriff?' asked the bartender. 'I reckon . . .' He stopped short, staring down at Corder's shirt. 'You lose your star?'

Corder tossed the drink down quickly. It exploded in his stomach and for a second, he grimaced before a welcome haze of warmth followed it. He sipped the second more slowly, swilling it around his mouth before swallowing it.

'That's right,' he said in a low voice. 'Jordan thinks I'm gettin' too old and feeble.' The bitterness in his tone was clearly audible.

'Shame,' muttered the bartender, wiping the counter with a wet cloth. 'I always had you figgered as a good man.'

'That ain't what Jordan thinks.' Corder poured a third slug of the liquor into his glass. Anger was still burning deep inside him, hot fury that threatened to boil over at any moment.

For over ten years he'd done all that the rancher had

asked of him, had carried out all of Jordan's dirty work. Even when, at times, it went against the grain. Now he had been tossed out to pasture and all for one mistake.

Leaning across the counter, he asked in low tones:

'Any o' Dancroft's men come in here?'

The other shook his head. 'Ain't seen any for quite a while, not since that trouble with the railroad.'

The news came as no surprise to Corder but already a plan was forming inside his scheming mind; a way of getting back at Jordan for what he'd done.

After two more drinks, he stepped away from the bar, swaying a little. He knew what he was planning could be dangerous but the boiling fury in his mind refused to go away. One way or another, Jordan was going to pay for this day's work.

He went along to where his mount was tethered and pulled himself awkwardly into the saddle. He rode slowly along the street, occasionally throwing a wary glance over his shoulder. So far, no one seemed to be taking much notice of him.

When he gained the shelter of the rocky ledge where the trail forked, he reined up and sat for several minutes scanning the street. He made to ride on, then swung his gaze back. He recognized Jordan at once as the rancher stepped out of the jailhouse.

Sanders was beside him. A second later Jordan raised a hand and pointed in his direction. Cursing, Corder jerked on the reins and put his horse to the Lazy W trail. It was possible Jordan had just guessed his intention, or more likely had spotted him through the office window. But he knew that if the rancher caught up with him he was a dead man. Jordan could not allow him to live and spill everything he knew.

Raking spurs along the mount's flanks, he spurred it along the rocky trail, riding at breakneck speed through the narrow canyon before putting the horse to the steep upgrade. At the far end were the pine-bordered slopes.

A shot shattered the silence at his back. Shaking violently, he managed to twist in the saddle and look behind him. The rider was just visible, halfway along the canyon.

At first, he thought it was Jordan pursuing him but, squinting against the bright sunlight, he recognized Sanders. He was still out of range of the other's gun but the man was gaining rapidly on him.

Desperately, he tried to urge more speed from his mount. Somehow, he had to reach the comparative safety of the Lazy W ranch. Once there, he might have a chance of staying alive.

Another shot sounded and this time he distinctly heard the wicked hum of the slug close to his head. Crouching low, ignoring everything but the need to stay ahead of Sanders, he entered the trees with sweat half-blinding him.

Through blurred vision, he searched desperately for any place where he could get off the trail and get the drop on the man following him. But there was nowhere. The thickly tangled underbrush beneath the trees afforded no entry.

By now, his mount was tiring; flecks of foam were flying from its mouth. A little voice at the back of his mind told him he wasn't going to make it, that he'd been a fool even to consider trying to get word to

Dancroft and that marshal of Jordan's intentions.

Then, up ahead of him, he caught sight of the ranch house less than a quarter of a mile away. He pulled his gun from leather, twisted and sent a couple of shots along the trail at his back, hoping to slow Sanders down.

There was no sign of the rider but he could hear the sound of hoofbeats quite distinctly and knew there were only scant seconds left before Sanders came within range.

He was just inside the courtyard when the shot came from the trees at his back. The slug took him between the shoulder blades, knocking him forward in the saddle. For a moment, he hung there, struggling to keep a tight grip on the reins. Then his hold loosened and he fell sideways into the dirt.

Among the trees, Sanders paused, saw Corder go down and lie still. Then he turned his mount and rode swiftly back along the trail.

The sound of the shot brought Anne and Rick running to the door. In an instant, they saw the riderless horse and then the body lying beside it.

Rick sprinted forward and went down on one knee beside the figure. He stared down at the flaccid features.

'It's Corder,' he said tersely. 'Shot in the back.'

'Corder?' Dancroft had come up and was peering over Rick's shoulder. Through tight lips, he asked: 'Is he dead?'

Rick felt for the pulse and in the same moment, Corder's eyes flicked open. His lips moved but for a long moment no sound came out.

'Who did this, Corder?' Rick asked. 'Was it Jordan?'

With an effort, Corder gave an almost imperceptible shake of his head. 'It was Sanders. I . . . I came to warn you. Jordan has men out to kill Wesley. He'll never reach here alive.'

'Why are you tellin' us all this?' Dancroft spoke with naked suspicion in his voice. 'Ain't like you to go against Jordan.'

Ignoring Dancroft's question, Rick said sharply: 'You got any idea where they intend to hit the stage?'

A long sigh came from Corder's slack lips. For a moment, Rick thought he was dead but then his lips moved again. 'Twin Peaks. Along the trail from Denver. Five of 'em. I . . .'

His voice trailed away. There was a faint rattle in his throat and his head fell to one side. His whole body loosened.

'He's dead,' Rick muttered, getting to his feet. 'But why did he come here to warn us?'

'Mebbe to deliberately throw you off the track,' Anne suggested. 'Can you trust anything he says?'

'Somehow, I guess I can. Whatever happened in town, he knew he was dyin'. There was no reason for him to lie.'

Dancroft bent closer. 'What do you make of this?' He pointed to where the other's shirt had been ripped when Jordan had torn the star off.

'Somehow, I had a feelin' something like this might happen. Jordan don't like men who make mistakes and don't carry out his orders. When Corder failed to take us in that must've really riled Jordan.'

'So Sanders must be the new sheriff in Twin Forks,' Anne murmured.

'I guess so.' Rick nodded. 'Reckon we were lucky Corder made it this far. I now know where those killers intend to hit that stage.'

'You goin' to try to stop 'em?' Dancroft asked.

'I'm certainly goin' to try.'

Rick had ridden for close on two days, pushing the stallion at a punishing pace along the Denver trail, sleeping for only a couple of hours during the night. After passing through Twin Peaks canyon, he now sat his mount on a high promontory watching for any sign of movement.

He did not have long to wait. Against the white backdrop of the alkali, he spotted the cloud of dust. Evidently the stage had run into no trouble since leaving Denver. He tossed his cigarette butt into the dust and started along the steep downgrade.

The stage was rattling along at a good pace and he could make out the figure of the driver seated high on the box. He reached the trail a short distance in front, stood his mount squarely in the middle of the trail, and raised his right hand.

For a moment, he thought the driver wasn't going to stop, possibly believing he was a decoy for other men hiding among the rocks on either side. Then the other must have seen he held no gun in his hand. He hauled back sharply on the reins.

The stage came to a halt less than ten yards away. Still cautious, the grizzled oldster reached sideways for the shotgun he had stacked beside him.

'There's no need for that scattergun,' Rick called loudly. 'But you may have to use it soon.'

'Just who are you, mister?' The driver glanced nervously from one side of the trail to the other. After a moment, he seemed satisfied that Rick was alone.

'I'm a federal marshal,' Rick moved his jacket slightly, showing the star. 'There's a bunch o' men waiting somewhere ahead intendin' on holding up this stage and kill one o' your passengers.'

'And who might that be?'

'Judge Wesley.'

'And how do you know all this?' The stage door opened and a tall man dressed in a black frock-coat and hat stepped down and stood facing Rick. A moment later, a broad smile spread over the judge's face.

'Rick Farnam,' he exclaimed, stepping forward and shaking hands. 'I got your message in Denver. Some trouble in Twin Forks, I gather.'

'There ain't no time to discuss it here, Judge,' Rick said quickly. 'This *hombre* Jordan has sent a bunch of his men to make sure you never make it there. I rode out to warn you.'

Wesley's right hand moved slightly as he drew aside his coat. He wore a gunbelt about his waist.

'Then I recokn they're goin' to discover I still know how to use these guns,' he said grimly.

Rick peered up at the stage. 'Any other passengers who might prove handy if they do hit the stage?'

'Just two,' Wesley replied. 'Come from back East. Look like businessmen to me. I doubt if either of 'em has used a gun before.'

Rick's eyes narrowed slightly. The thought had come to him that perhaps these men were working with Jordan. The rancher had often made it known that he was in with others intent on rich pickings from beef shipped to the north, men who didn't care what brand was on the steers just so long as they fetched a good price in the markets.

'Mind if I ride with you?' he asked.

'Glad to have you,' Wesley nodded and climbed back inside. 'What about your mount?'

'He'll follow. I'll hitch him to the back o' the stage. With luck those killers will figger he's a spare in case one o' the others throws a shoe.'

Two minutes later the stage was on its way again, rattling and bumping over the uneven ground.

'You got any idea where they mean to jump the stage?' Wesley asked.

'Up ahead, where the trail runs between those hills yonder. We'd better be ready. These killers don't mean to leave any witnesses.' He stared directly at the two men seated opposite.

Both were nervous, florid-faced men, neither of whom had ever come to this frontier territory before and were almost certainly wishing they had never done so.

Rick gave a grim smile.

'I'd advise both of you gentlemen to keep your heads down,' he said. 'These gunhawks mean business.'

Swallowing agitatedly, one said hoarsely:

'They told us in Denver there was no trouble now.'

'Guess they forgot to mention there are still men out here willin' to sell their guns to whoever pays most,' Wesley remarked drily. 'This country ain't been tamed yet, not by a long way.'

Rick nodded to the judge. 'You watch that side. I'll

take care of this,' he said harshly.

The other two passengers shrank back into their seats as Rick drew his Colt and waited, watching the trail ahead as they neared the rearing peaks in the distance.

'Keep an eye on the trail yonder. They could hit us without warnin',' he yelled to the driver.

'I'll be ready for 'em with this scattergun,' came the reply. 'Ain't the first time the stage has been held up.'

Within two minutes, the hills shut off all sunlight and they were in deep shadow. Rick waited tensely. Still there was no sign of any ambush. Had Corder been mistaken, or had he been lying even though he knew that death was only minutes away?

The next moment a gunshot shattered the stillness. It came from just in front of the stage, followed immediately by two others and then the pounding of hoofbeats on the stony ground. Seconds later, there came the unmistakable sound of the shotgun.

The driver yelled a warning but it was lost on Rick as he sighted on three men who came riding swiftly along the bottom of the slope. His first shot took one of the riders in the chest, pitching him from the saddle. Another horse and rider crashed through the trees. On the other side of the stage Wesley was firing swiftly at the other two bushwhackers.

A couple of slugs hammered into the stage close to Rick's head, forcing him to move back quickly. Steadying himself against the door, he drew a bead on a second man but missed as the stage hit a rock and threw him heavily to one side.

By the time he had righted himself, the riders had reached the stage, pacing their mounts alongside it.

One man bent to grab at the door and open it, holding himself sideways in the saddle. Pushing himself against the opposite seat, Rick twisted, bringing up the Colt in a single, fluid motion.

He had a fragmentary glimpse of a bearded face, black hair blowing wildly in the wind. He squeezed the trigger and saw the bullet take the man in the throat before he could fire. With a gurgling moan, the man slumped forward, his gun clattering into the dust. A moment later, he fell from his mount and the horse went running ahead.

'How are you doin' your side, Judge,' Rick called.

'I got one o' the critters,' the judge replied. 'Can't see any sign o' the other but I'm sure I didn't hit him.'

'Means there are still two of 'em around somewhere. I don't reckon they'll leave until you're dead.'

The driver had given the startled horses their heads and now the stage was pounding along the narrow trail, swaying precariously from side to side. Glancing through the small opening in the top of the stage, Rick called:

'You all right up there?'

'Sure thing, Marshal.'

'Can you see anythin' of those other two gunhawks?'

There was a pause and Rick guessed the driver was scanning the terrain on either side of the trail. Then:

'Nope. You reckon they weren't expectin' this kinda reception and they've pulled out?'

'That ain't likely. They're still around, probably trailin' us through those trees yonder, waitin' until we're out in the open.'

'That would be a danged fool thing to do. We could

spot 'em miles away.'

Rick sat back and thrust cartridges into the spent chambers of his Colt. He noticed that Wesley was doing the same. Across from them the other two passengers watched without saying anything. Both were hanging desperately on to the sides of the stage as it bumped and swayed along the trail.

Eyes still alert for any sign of danger, Rick said slowly without turning his head:

'Either of you gentlemen goin' to Twin Forks to see Ed Jordan?'

From the corner of his eye, he noticed the look that passed between them. Then one said tautly:

'Our business is with Mr Jordan. Why do you ask?'

Grimly, Rick replied: 'Because he's the one who sent these men to hold up the stage. I guessed from your clothing you're from somewhere back East and I doubt if you'd be interested in any o' the other ranchers.'

The second man spoke up.

'An associate of ours recently went to that town to take over the bank there.'

'Jepson. So he's in with Jordan too.'

Licking his dry lips, the first man said:

'I don't understand. From what you're intimating, Marshal, you're suggesting that Mr Jordan is acting outside the law in some respect.'

Staring directly at him, Rick said tersely:

'I've only been in Twin Forks for a few days but I've already got sufficient proof against Jordan to hang him. He's aimin' to take over the entire town, force the smaller ranchers off their land, and he's tryin' to build a branch line from the railroad across Indian land.'

'That's difficult to believe,' began the other. 'We've always thought that he—'

He broke off at a sudden yell from the driver.

'Behind us, Marshal, and gainin' on us fast.'

Rick flung himself down against the door. The remaining two hellions had evidently headed for the shelter of the trees when their three companions had been shot down. Both had their guns drawn and a moment later a fusillade of shots struck the rear of the coach.

'Get your heads down,' Rick called to the two passengers, still sitting rigidly in their seats.

As one, the men threw themselves on to the floor, crouching down as more gunfire erupted. Pressing his lips tightly together, Rick thrust his head out of the window. A bullet hummed like an angry insect close to his head. Swiftly, he loosed off a couple of shots and saw one of the men jerk violently in the saddle.

Somehow the gunman remained upright, still clutching the reins, head low. Now, with the stage rocking and swaying violently, it was difficult to take proper aim. Another slug tore at the brim of his hat as the riders closed in.

Knowing he was putting himself in line for a bullet, Rick forced calmness into his mind, remaining exposed as he deliberately took aim. The riders were now less than twenty feet behind the stage. The man who had fired at him was already lining up his Colt for a killing shot.

Very gently, Rick squeezed the trigger at almost exactly the same time as the other. Time seemed to move in slow motion. He saw the other sway as the slug took him in the chest. Somehow, even above the roar of his own gun, he distinctly heard the dull click as the rider's hammer fell on an empty chamber.

Then the man was gone from the saddle, his mount still plunging forward, kicking up the dust, while its rider lay in a crumpled heap in the middle of the trail. Swiftly, the body disappeared into the distance.

Instinctively, Rick swung the Colt to cover the last man but there was no need for him to fire. Wesley fired two more shots in rapid succession and both went home.

Wesley pulled himself back into his seat with a grim smile on his lips. 'Reckon I haven't lost my touch, Rick,' he said harshly. He glanced down at the two men crouched on the floor. 'You can get up now. From what I've heard from the marshal here, once we reach Twin Forks I guess you'll have to make a decision as to your business deals with Jordan. Could be you're puttin' in stakes with the wrong man.'

CHAPTER NINE

TRAIL'S END

Forty-eight hours later, the stage rolled into Twin Forks. There had been no further incidents along the trail and the early afternoon sun beat down like an inferno on the town as the driver brought the stage to a halt in front of the depot halfway along the street.

Throughout the last stretch of the journey, Rick had ridden alongside, keeping a sharp lookout for any more of Jordan's men, knowing that the rancher might have gunmen watching the trail in case anything had gone wrong.

There was a small bunch of men standing on the boardwalk just in front of the long wooden building. Looking down, Rick recognized several of the townsfolk. A few moments later someone pushed his way roughly through them. Rick saw the expression of shocked surprise which gusted over Jordan's fleshy features, then the rancher controlled himself almost at once.

'You're under arrest, Farnam,' Jordan grated harshly. 'I didn't think you'd be such a fool as to ride back into town.' He spun swiftly as Sanders came running along the boardwalk.

'Nobody's under arrest except on my say-so.' Wesley stepped down from the stage. 'Five men bushwhacked us near Twin Peaks. Reckon they wanted someone on the stage dead. Since I understand these two men who travelled with us are business friends o' yours from back East, that leaves only me.'

Jordan swallowed thickly. Quite suddenly, he seemed to have lost most of his bluster.

'I know nothin' about any stage hold-ups,' he said, jerking the words out. 'There ain't nothin' to connect me with what happened.'

He swung round to stare at Rick. 'All I know is that this marshal has thrown in his lot with a wanted killer. I reckon Sheriff Sanders here can corroborate that.'

'That's true, Judge,' Sanders affirmed. 'He . . .'

Wesley's face did not change.

'The last time I was here, Corder was sheriff. What happened to him?'

Before Rick could say anything, Jordan broke in harshly:

'He rode up to the Lazy W spread to bring in Clint Dancroft who's wanted for killin' three Sioux braves and Jeb Dressler, the lawyer. And we have an independent witness to testify that this lawman was with Dancroft when Dressler was shot. Corder never came back. My guess is that either Dancroft or this man killed him.'

'Then I guess I'll have to do some investigatin'

myself,' Wesley said coldly.

Jordan's eyes narrowed at that remark.

'Seems to me you're exceedin' your jurisdiction, Judge,' he said thickly. 'Your job is only to preside over a trial and pass sentence on anyone found guilty of a crime.'

A grim flicker of a smile touched Wesley's lips as he shook his head.

'My job is to get at the truth, Mr Jordan, and that's exactly what I aim to do.'

Jordan made to speak again, then thought better of it. He clamped his lips together into a straight line, signalled to Sanders, and strode off along the boardwalk.

Wesley watched the two men depart, then turned to Rick.

'You reckon I could get me a mount? I'm goin' to ride out to the Lazy W ranch and ask a few questions o' this man Dancroft. Then I suppose I have to check on this affair with the Sioux.'

'Sure. You'll pick one up at the livery stables yonder.' Rick jerked a thumb along the street. 'I also think you should stay at the ranch for the time bein'. My guess is that it won't be healthy to stay in any place in town.'

'Just what I was thinkin' after what happened on the way here.'

The shadows were lengthening as they arrived at the ranch. Both Dancroft and Anne were on the veranda as they rode up. Anne came forward to meet them. She glanced at Rick.

'I was worried when you didn't get back some time

ago,' she said softly. There was a warm glow on her face which Rick noticed at once and he felt it stir some long-forgotten emotions deep within him. 'I thought you might have been . . .'

'Killed by that bunch o' gunslingers?'

She gave a little nod but said nothing more.

Her father came forward.

'This is Judge Wesley,' said Rick. 'Like we figgered, Jordan did his best to have him killed before he got to town. I think this would be the best place for him to stay for a while. Two o' Jordan's associates were on the stage with us.'

'And you think Jordan's goin' to try again?' Without waiting for a reply, Dancroft turned to Wesley. 'You're welcome to stay here, Judge. I just hope that, with your help, we can rid this territory of Jordan and his hired killers.'

'From what little I've seen, you're not goin' to find that easy,' Wesley remarked. 'There's not much 1 can do to help except make sure that the right men are brought to justice.'

Anne went into the house and through into the kitchen. Motioning them to chairs, Dancroft said soberly:

'I've spent the last couple o' days ridin' round the other spreads talkin' to everyone.'

'Any of 'em willin' to throw in their hand with us against Jordan?' Rick asked.

Dancroft nodded. 'Seems that word you were on your way has got around, Judge. Before, they were all scared o' Jordan and his bunch and wouldn't dare do anythin'. Now it seems they've changed their minds.'

Wesley sat quite still, drumming with his fingers on the table. Then he spoke.

'One thing is certain. Jordan was bankin' on killin' me on that stage. He's also lost five men in that attempt. Now he's bein' pushed to the limit and he's got to act fast unless he wants to lose everythin'.'

'Meanin' we have to hit him first before he's ready,' Rick muttered.

'Exactly. And the sooner, the better. How soon can you have all of your men together?'

A grim expression on his face, Dancroft replied:

'I reckon they could all be here by tomorrow night.'

'How many?'

Dancroft scratched his chin. 'Thirty, mebbe forty, men. But you got to remember, these ain't hired gunmen. These are just cattlemen.'

'And Jordan?'

'Hard to say. He's been bringin' in men all the time and I guess Sanders, the new sheriff, will put in with him. Perhaps a few o' the townsfolk whom Corder used as a posse.'

At that moment Anne came in with the coffee. She put it down on the table and seated herself in the chair by the window.

As he sipped the coffee, Wesley said tautly:

'Get those men here. All we have to figger out now is where best to hit Jordan? Where's his spread?'

'It joins on to mine,' Dancroft explained. 'Runs all o' the way to the north and west o' town.'

'Then it's unlikely he'll be there. My guess is he'll most likely be in town, buyin' his men drinks before he makes his move.'

Leaning forward, Rick said softly: 'Then I suggest we split our forces, move in from both ends o' town. That way, we've got 'em pinned down.'

Both men nodded in agreement.

As he left the sheriff's office, both hands clasped behind his back, Jordan tried to control the anger burning deep inside him. Now was the time to think clearly and rationally. Things were going from bad to worse and for the moment, he could do nothing about it. The colour showing high in his cheeks, he chewed on the cigar between his thick lips. At last he swung on Sanders.

'How the hell did this happen? I send out five men, all fast with a gun, to take that stage – and what happens? All of 'em get killed and Wesley is still alive.'

'Someone talked,' Sanders put in, keeping his voice even. 'Otherwise, how did Farnam know about those men and where it was goin' to happen?'

Jordan's face assumed a thoughtful look. For a moment, he remained silent, then he grated:

'Only one way he could've known. Corder.'

'But that ain't possible. I shot him before he could talk.'

'Sure you shot him.' Jordan clenched his fists by his sides. 'But you never made sure he was dead before Dancroft got to him. I knew we should've finished him off before he got out there.'

'So what are you goin' to do now with Wesley in the territory? And don't forget those Sioux still out yonder.'

'I ain't forgetting 'em. But for the moment, I've got more important matters on my mind. Matters that can't wait. I have to get rid of Wesley and that marshal. Once that's done, I'll take care o' the Sioux.'

Hardened as he was, Sanders felt a little prickle at the back of his neck at the savage fury in the other's tone.

Jordan lit a match and applied it to the end of his cigar. He blew smoke into the air. Thinly, he said:

'How many men can you get to ride against the Lazy W? I need men I can trust.'

Pursing his lips, Sanders thought for a moment.

'Ten, perhaps a dozen.'

'Good. It'll take me a day or so to round up all o' mine. There won't be much moon tomorrow night. I'll bring my boys into town and then we'll finish Dancroft for good.' As he turned towards the door, he added: 'And this time there'll be no mistakes. I'll be here to make sure o' that.'

Standing on the veranda, Rick looked out over the courtyard where the riders were gathered in the darkness. It was impossible to estimate their number exactly but he reckoned there were close on forty men there.

They rode out a few minutes later with the cold chill of the night riding with them. Somewhere ahead lay Twin Forks and the final showdown with Jordan. Each man rode with his own thoughts and there was no conversation until they came in sight of the wide canyon where the trail led on into town.

Here Rick held up his hand and halted them.

'If we're lucky, we've got Jordan and his men holed up in town,' he said. 'And so far, they ain't expectin' us.'

Nodding to Judge Wesley and Dancroft, he went on:

'You take half o' the men straight on into this end o' town. I'll swing around with the others until we hit the railroad.'

'We'll give you ten minutes and then we move in,' Wesley said. 'By that time you should be in position to cut 'em off.'

With a gesture to the men who were to follow him, Rick cut off the trail towards the north. Soon, they spotted the cattle-pens, just visible in the darkness. Further on were the lights of the town.

Moving well clear of the town, they set their mounts at a gallop, riding across the flat grass country before swinging back again to where the railroad depot stood out as a black shadow to their left.

One of the riders uttered a low warning murmur, pointing. Still present, as if painted against the backdrop, the long line of Sioux warriors sat their ponies.

'They're no danger to us,' Rick called softly. 'The only enemy here is Jordan.'

'There's talk there are soldiers in the town,' muttered another man.

'There are,' Rick affirmed. 'They may throw in their lot with Jordan. He seems to be in cahoots with their captain. On the other hand, they may stay out of it until it's finished.'

Past the railroad depot they edged their mounts towards the edge of town. In front of them the street began, less than twenty feet away. Pushing his gaze along it, Rick searched for any sign of Jordan and Sanders.

Tinny music drifted from the saloons and it was soon evident that all were crowded with men. Apart from these, the rest of the town seemed dark and oddly deserted. A little finger of ice brushed along Rick's spine as he scanned the scene. The feeling in the air was like that just before a storm broke.

For a moment he sat there, puzzled. He could imagine no way the townsfolk could know of their coming for a showdown. The men sitting their mounts behind him were silent and watchful.

The ordinary townsfolk were all inside, off the street, almost certainly behind bolted doors as if sensing the imminence of something big about to break. Then it came to him. Jordan had also picked this night to make his strike and now he was in one of those saloons, getting his men all fired up for the attack, almost certainly against the Lazy W ranch, to rid himself of everyone who posed a threat to him.

Scarcely had the thought crossed his mind than two figures emerged from the nearest saloon and made their way across the street to one of the others. One glance was sufficient to tell him who they were. Ed Jordan and Sanders.

The man next to him raised his Winchester but Rick knocked it away and grabbed his arm.

'Not yet,' he hissed. 'When the other bunch move in from the far end, we do the same.'

The minutes passed with an agonizing slowness. Then, off in the distance, there came a loud yell followed by the pounding of hoofbeats.

'Right. Take the nearest saloon and keep under cover.' Rick stepped down from the saddle and sprinted for the boardwalk opposite the saloon. Crouching down beside him, the rest of the men drew their guns and aimed them at the wide windows.

A second later, one of the windows shattered as it was struck from inside by a gunbutt. A volley of gunfire sent shrieking echoes along the street. Clearly, the men inside had been alerted by the sound of horses and it had not taken them long to recognize their danger.

Swiftly, Rick aimed and loosed off a couple of shots, saw the indistinct shadow at the window jerk and fall back out of sight. Wood splintered as another volley rang out from the men beside him.

More firing came from the direction of the other two saloons as Dancroft and Wesley closed in with their men.

Beside Rick, one of the men muttered: 'How do you figure on gettin' them outa there, Marshal? Seems they have plenty of ammunition and that wall is pretty thick.'

Rick thought it over for a few seconds, then reached a decision.

'Six o' you men come with me. The rest of you keep 'em pinned down.'

He lifted himself to his feet and darted along the boardwalk with the men close on his heels. Keeping his head down, he ran across the street to the dark alley beside the sheriff's office.

Once inside, he led the men along the backs of the buildings to the rear of the saloon. There were no doors there, just a couple of windows. Hoping that the noise would not be heard above the racketing din of gunfire, he swung the Colt, smashing the glass to splinters.

Once inside, he helped the others over the ledge. This was obviously a dressing-room for the dance-girls.

Before he could reach the door it burst open and three of the girls rushed in.

One made to scream as they spotted him, then choked the sound down as Rick lifted his Colt.

'Don't make a sound, any of you,' he said warningly. Showing the star on his shirt, he added: 'Those men in there are killers. Just stay here outa sight and you won't get hurt.'

He moved out into the narrow corridor and made his way swiftly to the door at the far end. He opened it a couple of inches and found himself at the end of the bar. A few feet away the bartender was crouched behind it as bullets hammered across the room.

Keeping down, he edged along the bar, then risked a quick look. Jordan's men were along the far wall, keeping well down below the windows. Sensing him, the bartender made a sudden move, then halted his hand as Rick levelled the Colt on him.

'All right, you men,' Rick called, raising his voice to make himself heard above the din. 'Drop your guns.'

Several of the gunhawks whirled. Stunned shock showed on their faces. Then one of them called out. 'You ain't takin' us, lawman.' The man fired from the hip and Rick ducked as the slug tore a piece out of the bar an inch from his head.

Gritting his teeth, he aimed and fired in the same fluid motion. The man who had fired pitched forward on to his face. Within seconds, the men with Rick opened up and within five minutes it was all over.

Warily, Rick went out into the street, signalling to the men opposite. Stray shots continued to come from within the two saloons but it soon appeared that

Jordan's men were finished.

Dancroft came running over. There was a smear of blood on his sleeve.

'We got 'em all except for Jordan and Sanders. Somehow, they got out o' the back. They're headed for the railroad depot.'

'You men stay here.' Rick spun on his heel and ran along the boardwalk, thrusting shells into his gun. In front of him, the depot was a black silhouette. There was no movement in the darkness as he approached it.

Then a sudden sound caught his attention. It was the faint exhalation of breath, the sound a man made when he wasn't sure where his pursuer was. Moments later, Rick pinpointed it off to his right.

'You're finished, Jordan,' he said, pressing himself hard against the wall of the depot. 'This is the end o' the trail for you and—'

A sudden spurt of gunfire pierced the darkness but Rick had already moved and the slug hit the wall where he had been standing a moment earlier. Then his own gun threw death into the shadows. The man in the shadows stumbled, then dropped to his knees, the gun falling from his hand.

Bending, Rick glanced down and saw that it was Sanders. He straightened up, made to turn and caught the soft sound behind him a moment before he glimpsed the man at his back. Instinctively, he twisted to one side and the gunbutt caught him a glancing blow on the shoulder.

Pain jarred agonizingly along his arm and the Colt fell from his fingers. Forcing himself to turn, he stared at Jordan.

'It's you who're finished, Farnam,' rasped the rancher. 'I could have shot you in the back just now but I want you to face me when you die.'

'You won't get away, Jordan,' Rick muttered. 'All o' your killers are either dead or in the jail by now.'

'I'll get away.' Jordan jerked his head slightly. 'I've got a horse yonder. I'll be miles away before Dancroft and those others get here. It was foolish of you to come after Sanders and me alone but I reckon that was your sense o' justice. Now I'm goin' to send you to hell.'

Slowly, the rancher raised his Colt, levelling it on Rick's chest. 'Ain't no good yellin' for your friends back there. They're too busy roundin' up my—'

Jordan broke off abruptly. His mouth dropped slackly open but no further sound came out. Stepping forward, Rick made a grab for the rancher's gun but there was no need. Jordan's legs gave way. His hand reached out for the wall in a last despairing effort to keep himself upright.

Then he fell forward and lay still. Staring down in the dimness, Rick saw the arrow in the rancher's back. A moment later, a shadow moved silently out of the darkness.

'This white man was evil.' Grey Eagle looked at Rick over Jordan's lifeless body. 'He deserved to die.'

The sun was lifting over the wooded slopes two days later as Rick stepped out into the courtyard of the Lazy W ranch. Wesley was there in deep conversation with Dancroft. They both turned as he came up to them.

'I guess you'll be ridin' back to Denver, Rick,' Dancroft said.

Throwing a quick glance at the sky, Rick nodded. 'Reckon my work here is finished now. With Jordan dead, I think you should talk with those two men from back East and then have a parley with the Sioux. Could be that branch o' the railroad is a good thing for the town if all of the ranchers chipped in and finished it.'

There was silence for a moment, then Wesley said slowly:

'Might be this town also needs someone to uphold the law. Someone who ain't in the pay of greedy men like Jordan.'

'If you're meanin' me, I'm a federal marshal. You sayin' I should give that up and take on the job o' sheriff?'

Wesley gave a faint smile. 'I was a federal marshal before I became a circuit judge, though there ain't many who know that. Think about it. There comes a time when a man who rides a lonely trail comes to a fork. When that happens, if he's a wise man, he should leave it to fate or . . .' He threw a meaningful glance in Anne's direction where she stood a few feet away, 'or other circumstances, to choose the right way for him.'

'I . . . we . . . want you to stay, Rick,' she said softly. She was smiling at him and there was a deep, warm glow at the back of her eyes.

Wesley held out his hand.

'I'll take that star back to Denver once I've passed sentence on those polecats we've got in the jail. The next time I come to Twin Forks, I expect to find you sheriff here.'